Puppet Killer

To an outsider, the scene backstage would have seemed chaotic, as many people rushed to and fro, each on his own errand. If anyone was asked later if someone had passed through carrying a samisen, all they would recall was a figure dressed entirely in black, with a full hood that concealed his face. That, of course, merely marked him as one of the many puppeteers in the troupe.

Showing no hesitation, the thief mounted the small staircase that led to the prop room. It was cluttered with doll-size umbrellas, swords, lanterns, flutes, tea sets, carts—everything that might be needed in a world inhabited by puppets. Here, where no one but puppets watched, he carefully removed one of the samisen's three long strings. He tested its strength, pulling the ends taut between his hands. Made of braided silk, the string was tough enough to withstand any pressure that might be applied to it. Wrapped around another man's neck, it could cut off his breath and resist his efforts to claw free. The thief's hands tingled with anticipation. He could already feel the satisfaction it would give him. He covered his mouth, stifling the laugh that wanted to burst forth.

OTHER BOOKS YOU MAY ENJOY

The Boy Who Saved Baseball	John H. Ritter
The Demon in the Teahouse	Dorothy and Thomas Hoobler
The Ghost in the Tokaido Inn	Dorothy and Thomas Hoobler
Haunted	Judith St. George
The Hound of the Baskervilles	Sir Arthur Conan Doyle
In Darkness, Death	Dorothy and Thomas Hoobler
Shakespeare's Scribe	Gary Blackwood
Shakespeare's Spy	Gary Blackwood
The Shakespeare Stealer	Gary Blackwood
The Westing Game	Ellen Raskin

A Samurai Never Fears Death

A SAMURAI MYSTERY

DOROTHY & THOMAS HOOBLER

PUFFIN BOOKS

Published by the Penguin Group

Penguin Young Readers Group, 345 Hudson Street, New York, New York 10014, U.S.A.

Penguin Group (Canada), 90 Eglinton Avenue East, Suite 700, Toronto, Ontario, Canada M4P
2Y3 (a division of Pearson Penguin Canada Inc.)

Penguin Books Ltd, 80 Strand, London WC2R 0RL, England

Penguin Ireland, 25 St Stephen's Green, Dublin 2, Ireland (a division of Penguin Books Ltd)

Penguin Group (Australia), 250 Camberwell Road, Camberwell, Victoria 3124, Australia
(a division of Pearson Australia Group Pty Ltd)

Penguin Books India Pvt Ltd, 11 Community Centre, Panchsheel Park, New Delhi - 110 017, India

Penguin Group (NZ), 67 Apollo Drive, Rosedale, North Shore 0632, New Zealand
(a division of Pearson New Zealand Ltd.)

Penguin Books (South Africa) (Pty) Ltd, 24 Sturdee Avenue,
Rosebank, Johannesburg 2196, South Africa

Registered Offices: Penguin Books Ltd, 80 Strand, London WC2R 0RL, England

First published in the United States of America by Philomel,
a division of the Penguin Young Readers Group, 2007

Published by Puffin Books, a division of Penguin Young Readers Group, 2008

1 3 5 7 9 10 8 6 4 2

THE LIBRARY OF CONGRESS HAS CATALOGED THE PHILOMEL EDITION AS FOLLOWS:

Hoobler, Dorothy.

A samurai never fears death / Dorothy and Thomas Hoobler.

p.   cm.—(A samurai mystery)

Summary: Returning home to investigate the possible connection of his family's tea shop with
smugglers, Seikei, now a samurai in eighteenth-century Japan, becomes involved in murder at
a local puppet theater and saving the life of his sister's accused boyfriend.

ISBN: 978-0-399-24609-8 (hc)

1. Japan—History—Tokugawa period, 1600–1868—Juvenile fiction.
[1. Japan—History—Tokugawa period, 1600–1868—Fiction. 2. Samurai—Fiction.
3. Puppet theater—Fiction. 4. Mystery and detective stories.]
I. Hoobler, Thomas. II. Title. III. Series: Hoobler, Dorothy. Samurai mystery.
PZ7.H76227Sam2007   [Fic]—dc22   2006014264

Puffin Books ISBN 978-0-14-241208-4

Printed in the United States of America

To our daughter, Ellen.

CONTENTS

Prologue 1

1. — Unspoken Thoughts 3

2. — Homecoming 10

3. — A Love Suicide 20

4. — A Swiftly Solved Case 31

5. — The Master of Heads 42

6. — Too Many Suspects 53

7. — Ojoji's Story 63

8. — Night Deliveries 75

9. — It Gets in Your Blood 84

10. — The Bleeding Head 94

11. — Case Closed—Almost 104

12. — The Meaning of the Play 115

13. — Looking for Goblins 124

14. — At Sea with Captain Thunder 132

15. — The Silk Seller 143

16. — The Captain's Offer 153

17. — The Killer Samurai   164

18. — The Secret of the Storage Room   174

19. — Judgment   187

20. — Authors' Note   197

A Samurai
Never Fears Death

PROLOGUE

Even if Tayo had not been deep in meditation, his blindness would have kept him from noticing when someone took his samisen. The thief knew enough to grasp the instrument around its neck so the strings would make no sound to alert the old musician. He slipped silently away, joining the others who were preparing for the day's performances.

To an outsider, the scene backstage would have seemed chaotic, as many people rushed to and fro, each on his own errand. If anyone was asked later if someone had passed through carrying a samisen, all they would recall was a figure dressed entirely in black, with a full hood that concealed his face. That, of course, merely marked him as one of the many puppeteers in the troupe.

Showing no hesitation, the thief mounted the small staircase that led to the prop room. It was cluttered with doll-size umbrellas, swords, lanterns, flutes, tea sets, carts—everything that might be needed in a world inhabited by puppets. Here, where no one but puppets watched, he carefully removed one of the samisen's three long strings. He tested its strength, pulling the ends taut between his hands. Made of braided silk, the string was tough enough to withstand any pressure that might be applied to it. Wrapped around another man's neck, it could cut off his breath and resist his efforts to claw free. The thief's hands tingled with anticipation. He could already feel the satisfaction it would give him. He covered his mouth, stifling the laugh that wanted to burst forth.

1 —
UNSPOKEN THOUGHTS

*Y*our family will think I treat you cruelly," Judge Ooka said.

Seikei was startled out of his thoughts. "No!" he protested. Then he asked, "Why do you think so?" for the judge always had good reason for anything he said.

They rode on horseback, nearing the end of a twelve-day journey up the Tokaido Road from Edo. Behind them rode Bunzo, the judge's trusted aide, and two other *samurai*. All three of them, Seikei knew, would not hesitate to sacrifice their lives to protect the judge from harm.

Fortunately, there had been no need to do so on this trip. The banner carried by one of the judge's men held the image of a hollyhock, marking them as samurai in the service of the *shogun,* the military ruler of Japan. Anyone foolish enough to interfere with them would almost certainly be condemning himself to a painful death, unless he were allowed to commit suicide first.

The judge, though he was empowered to do so, rarely imposed the death penalty on any of the criminals he tracked down. Nor did he appear harsh, with his Buddha-like girth and normally placid expression. Of course, Seikei knew, the judge's appearance could be deceiving, for it concealed a razor-sharp mind that could solve the most difficult of crimes.

"When your family sees your unhappy look," the judge said now, "they will conclude that you regret ever having wished to become a samurai. That can only be my fault, as your adopted father."

Seikei smiled, for now he understood that the judge was joking. He knew that Seikei had always wished to be a samurai—a desire that had seemed impossible, for he had been born into a family of tea merchants. Even though the tea business had enabled his father to provide well for his family (a fact that Seikei's father had continually pointed out to him), Seikei had not been consoled. Basho, the poet who was his personal hero, had been a samurai. All the glorious warriors whose lives were spent in pursuit of honor had been samurai.

From the time he could read, Seikei had studied the code of *bushido*—instead of learning the skill of the abacus, as his father had wished—but knowing the way of the warrior did not make him a samurai. Then, while traveling on this very road two years ago, Seikei had been witness to a crime. When the judge had arrived to investigate, Seikei had told him what he'd seen. The judge then sent him on a mission to join the *kabuki* troupe where the criminal was hiding. Seikei had carried out his task so well that the judge had granted Seikei's wish the only way possible: by adopting him and thus making him a member of a samurai family.

Adopting sons—especially by those who had no sons—was not unusual, but it was almost unheard of for a foster son to be raised from the lowly merchant class to samurai status. Seikei always tried to make sure the judge would have no cause to regret it. His first father, truth to tell, was also pleased by the turn of events. The tea business would eventually have been passed on to Seikei, the eldest son, even though his younger brother Denzaburo had a far better head for business.

It had been the thought of his original family that had caused Seikei's look of unhappiness. In a little while now, Seikei and the judge would arrive at Osaka, the city where Seikei had been born. He had not seen it since becoming the judge's son, and indeed he was not sure he wanted to. The judge was going there to investigate

5

reports that a gang of smugglers was operating in Osaka's seaport. Though Seikei had frequently proved useful in solving some other cases with the judge, he could hardly see how he might help this time.

The judge had nodded when Seikei expressed his doubts. "You are resourceful," the judge had replied, "and it is said that only someone born there understands how to get around Osaka."

That was true. The city had begun as a village on the delta of the Yodo, Aji, and several other rivers, where they flow into Osaka Bay at the eastern end of the great Inland Sea. As the town grew, the people had dug canals to connect the many waterways of the delta, and by now it was easier to get around the city by boat than on foot. It was said that there were more than a thousand bridges in the city, and only a native-born Osakan knew where most of them were. Many could not even be found on maps.

"At any rate," the judge had told Seikei, "this will be a good time for you to pay your respects to your family."

"You are my father now," said Seikei, stopping himself from adding, "and I have no desire to return to my first one."

"To be sure," replied the judge, "but you will always

owe a debt to your parents who gave you life and cared for you before I became your father."

Seikei hung his head, glad that the judge had not heard his unspoken thought. A samurai, he reminded himself, should always be aware of the duty he owes to others. He shouldn't have to be prodded into paying respect to those who deserve it.

The road curved around a grove of pine trees, and there, off in the distance, Seikei saw the unmistakable outlines of Osaka Castle rising high above the city. The walls were made of thousands of stones that had been brought by ship into Osaka Bay from all parts of Japan. It was said that a thousand ships a day arrived during the three years it took to build the castle.

As a boy, Seikei had often walked as close as he dared to stare at the castle and imagine what might go on behind those massive walls. He and his friends often speculated about the fabled Octopus Stone, said to be five times as tall as the tallest man and bearing the imprint of a giant octopus that had been caught in it when a volcano erupted beneath the sea. Now, Seikei would get to see it for himself, for the judge's mission would surely bring him into contact with the provincial governor, whose headquarters were inside the castle.

"Are we going there?" Seikei ventured to ask.

The judge sighed. "Sadly, I must," he said. "Did you know that a hundred thousand warriors once assembled inside the castle to defend it?"

"I have heard that," said Seikei.

"Well, today, there are said to be nearly that many officials inside—all of whom demand to be consulted and flattered by anyone with a plan of action."

Seikei nodded. "I will be glad to help in any way I can," he said, helpfully.

"The way you can best assist me," said the judge, "is to stay with your family, pay your respects to them, and find me the restaurant that serves the best *fugu* in Osaka."

"Pufferfish?" Seikei asked, dismayed. "But if fugu isn't prepared by a skilled chef, it can cause a swift and agonizing death."

"Exactly why the governor refuses to serve it inside Osaka Castle," said the judge. "He's a most cautious man. But you are intelligent and know the city well, and I trust that you will find a place that will allow me to enjoy the unparalleled sensation of eating fugu"—he closed his eyes, as if anticipating it already—"without, of course, the unpleasant after-effects."

Seikei blinked. He wanted to say, "No! I want to go inside the castle. I've never eaten fugu in my life, because my original father is at least as cautious as the governor. And the last thing I hoped to do in Osaka was sleep under his roof again."

But of course he said none of those things. He merely nodded to show that he understood and would carry out the judge's wishes.

When they came to the place where Seikei had to dismount and hire a small boat to carry him in a different direction, Bunzo stayed behind for a moment. As he tied Seikei's horse to his own, he spoke in a low voice: "You know, the one hundred thousand warriors who defended the castle were defeated and slaughtered to the last man."

Seikei shivered. He remembered the story.

"The judge will prevail in the castle," added Bunzo. "All you have to do is make sure that the fugu is properly prepared." He gave Seikei a look before he turned and rode off. Seikei understood the look. It meant, "If you don't, you will suffer the same fate as the one hundred thousand defenders of Osaka Castle."

2 –
HOMECOMING

*T*he tea shop appeared smaller than Seikei had remembered. The sign above the canal entrance still read KONOIKE EXCELLENT TEAS. He looked more closely. Had the sign been repainted? That must be Denzaburo's doing. Father would have avoided the expense. Thinking of that drew Seikei's eye to the small window just under the slanting tile roof on the second story—his window, in the room he had shared with his brother. How many times had Seikei looked out from there, hoping to see a group of samurai pass by, imagining that they would look every bit as brave, honorable, and skilled as the stories said. On this narrow little street along the canal, of course, warriors never traveled. Only occasionally did Seikei spy a few *ronin*—samurai with no masters—who were often little better than beggars. Father would give them some coins to make them go away without causing trouble.

Now, at last, a true samurai stepped from the boat onto the wet stone steps at the canal's edge, one who was a member of a family that served the shogun himself. Seikei smiled as he thought of what he had experienced since he had last seen the shop. Here stood a samurai who had faced death . . . well, twice anyway. A samurai who had even masqueraded for a brief time as the emperor. One who was the adopted son of Judge Ooka, the scourge of criminals throughout the land.

That was Seikei. Who would have believed it? Not even he himself, daydreaming out the window, would have thought such a thing could happen.

A young woman emerged from the doorway of the shop and began to sweep the front steps—angrily, as if she were trying to scrape a hole in the stone. He recognized her at once, but as she looked up and saw him staring at her, she frowned, as if she were wondering why he'd stopped there. Seikei had not told them he was coming.

Then Asako's face changed—for it was indeed Seikei's sister, two years older than he—and she stepped warily toward him, as if he were a strange creature that had somehow wandered here, searching for water or food. As she came closer, she seemed to grow more sure of herself. "So it is you," she said finally. She looked at his swords. "And you really are a samurai."

11

"Didn't Father tell you that I had been adopted by Judge Ooka?" Seikei asked. Even here they would have heard of the judge.

"Oh, he did," Asako replied, "but I never quite believed it. I thought he dumped you somewhere so that Denzaburo could take over the business."

Seikei felt disappointed. He'd expected more of a homecoming than this. But then, it had always been difficult to impress Asako. She was the shrewdest member of the family.

"Are Mother and Father inside?" Seikei asked. He realized as soon as he'd said it that they weren't his parents any longer, but it seemed awkward to call them anything else.

"Father has been ill," Asako replied. "We don't live above the shop any longer. We have a house in Dojima. He and Mother spend most of their time there. Denzaburo and I run the shop."

"I'm surprised Mother would leave here," said Seikei, "even for a nice neighborhood like Dojima. All of her old friends live on this street." He set down his traveling bag, which held only a few clothes. He had not thought to bring gifts, he realized.

"You're taller," commented Asako.

It was true. For the first time in his life, Seikei looked

down on her when they stood face-to-face. To him, that change almost seemed more important than becoming a samurai.

"Denzaburo is ambitious," Asako said. "He wanted to use the family rooms to expand the business."

"Father must have approved of that," said Seikei, but Asako did not reply. She turned and headed back inside, and he followed.

"I thought you might be married by now," Seikei said.

She turned and gave him a sharp look. "A girl as ugly as I am needs a large dowry."

Seikei had never thought of his sister as ugly. He gave her a sideways glance. She seemed even a bit pretty, as far as he could tell. She was plump, with a flat nose, and the back of her neck—the part that most appealed to men— looked shapely enough. "But Father must have enough money for your dowry," he said.

"Oh, he has it," she replied. "If you want to know the truth, Denzaburo needs me to help him run the shop. And it's he—" She stopped, for the door to the shop had opened, and Denzaburo stepped out, an impatient look on his face. He started to speak to Asako, but then saw Seikei.

Immediately Denzaburo dropped to his knees. "Honored brother!" he exclaimed, talking to the floor of the front porch. "May I still call you brother? If not, I apologize. We have long wondered if you would honor us with a visit."

Seikei was embarrassed. He found Denzaburo's reaction to his arrival even more disconcerting than Asako's.

She, on the other hand, merely walked around Denzaburo and into the shop. "Stop it, Denzaburo," she called back. "It's just Seikei."

Seikei put his hand awkwardly on Denzaburo's shoulder. "Please," he said, "just treat me as you always did." It occurred to Seikei as he said this that all he could remember of the old days was Denzaburo making fun of his admiration for samurai.

Nevertheless, Denzaburo rose to his feet and embraced Seikei as if they had always been the closest of friends. Seikei was silently pleased to note that his younger brother was still shorter than he was.

"Are you staying in Osaka long?" Denzaburo asked as he led Seikei inside.

"I'm not sure," Seikei said, looking around. Asako was right. Denzaburo had clearly expanded the business. There were many more barrels of tea in the front room now. Seikei walked around, looking at them. One of them had a label with a word he did not recognize. He lifted the lid, interested in what it might contain.

Denzaburo reached out to stop him, then remembered you weren't supposed to grab a samurai's arm. Instead, he pressed the lid down firmly. "Oh, don't bother yourself with that," he said, chuckling in an unconvincing attempt to pretend he was joking. "You're not a merchant anymore, remember?" He turned, calling loudly, "Asako? Why haven't you served our brother some tea?"

Immediately she appeared from the back, carrying a tray with cups and a steaming teapot. "Boiling water can't be hurried," she said, "even when a samurai is waiting." She set the tray down on the square table where Seikei's father used to entertain important customers. She had to clear away some papers and small bags that sounded as if coins were inside. Father would never have left such things on his guest table, Seikei thought.

Self-consciously he removed his two swords from his *obi* before sitting on the mat next to the table. The swords were the unmistakable badge of the samurai, and even Asako refrained from commenting as he arranged them on the floor next to him.

Seikei recognized the tea by its aroma even before he tasted it. So did Denzaburo. "Asako," he scolded, "this is not our best tea. You should serve a samurai—"

"No," said Seikei, holding up his hand. "Asako knew just what would please me most." He smiled at her and got a look of satisfaction in return. "This is the kind of tea that Mother served us as a treat on Boys' Day."

"It's flavored," Denzaburo said with an air of contempt he could not conceal.

"Yes," said Seikei, "but the flavor is of home."

He took his time as he sipped from the cup, holding it in both hands. Tea, he knew, can do many things, but this cup transported him back in time, to the days when the three of them were children. Father was just starting to become really successful, and everyone felt a sense of security and happiness. The taste of the tea almost restored the feeling that nothing would ever go wrong.

Asako had gone back to the kitchen and now returned with a plate of steaming dumplings. Seikei knew that when he bit into one, he would taste the fresh octopus meat that was inside. He did, and found it as succulent and delicious as ever.

"That reminds me," he said suddenly, his mouth full. "I'm supposed to find a place that serves fugu."

His sister and brother exchanged a glance. "Well," said Asako, "your tastes certainly have changed."

"Oh, no," protested Seikei. "These octopus dumplings are just what I wanted. But my father—my new father, the judge—wants to try some fugu while we're here."

Asako put her finger to her lips, and Seikei smiled in recognition. The gesture had been a habit of hers whenever someone did or said something she didn't like. "Tell him to forget it," she said. "No sense in tempting fate."

"Well, of course he would want a chef who knows how to remove the poisonous parts from the fish," said Seikei.

"Naturally," said Asako dryly. "Everyone does, and every chef assures you he can do it. But a few times a year you hear of someone who dies from eating fugu. All the knife has to do is slip just the tiniest bit and—" She grasped her neck, stuck out her tongue, and made a face as if choking to death. Seikei cringed, thinking of that happening to the judge.

"The best thing to do," Asako went on, "is to arrange to have a chef serve some other kind of fish, passing it off as fugu, because anyone who doesn't live in Osaka can't tell the difference."

"I couldn't do that," Seikei said, shocked at the thought of deceiving the judge. "Anyway, he would probably know it if they served a substitute. He is very clever."

Asako shrugged. "As you like," she said. "Where are you staying while you're here?"

"I thought I would stay here with you."

"That's impossible," Denzaburo broke in. Then, realizing he had spoken rudely, he added, "You would be welcome, but there is no room. Why not come to our new house? Father and Mother will be glad to see you."

Asako started to say something, Seikei noticed, but stopped herself.

"The judge thinks I am staying here," said Seikei. "If he sends for me, this is where the message will come."

"That will not be a problem," said Denzaburo. "I will send it on to you."

"So *you* are staying here?" Seikei asked.

"Only when we are expecting merchandise to arrive," Denzaburo replied.

"At night?" Guards patrolled the streets of the city at night and questioned anyone who was out late. No deliveries of any kind were made then.

Denzaburo spread his hands and gave a little laugh. "Some of the suppliers have their own ways of doing business."

It sounded very odd to Seikei, but before he could ask another question, Denzaburo said, "Let me show you something we always wanted to see when we were boys."

"What's that?"

"The *joruri* theater, the puppet show. Remember how when we begged Father to take us he always said the shows were too violent?"

Seikei couldn't help smiling. That was just what Father had said, many times.

"Since you left," Denzaburo went on, "I've begun attending a theater on Dotombori Street. We can go there now and afterward get a bite to eat. No fugu, though," he warned. "I'm not so foolish as to try that."

Seikei frowned. He felt that calling it foolish was slightly insulting to the judge.

Denzaburo, thinking that Seikei was hesitating for other reasons, urged, "Come along. Asako would like to go too," he said with a smirk and a look at their sister.

If Seikei had not known better, he would have thought Asako was blushing. Though he did not want to admit it, he was curious about the puppet theater. Everybody in Osaka always talked about it. He could look for a place that served fugu tomorrow.

"All right," he said. "Let's go."

3 —
A LOVE SUICIDE

As the three of them crossed the Ebisubashi Bridge, Seikei saw that this part of the city was busier than ever. The bridge was clogged with people carrying bundles or pulling small carts loaded with goods. There were hardly any samurai to be seen, unlike in Edo, where nearly all the residents were samurai or servants in a samurai household.

Anything, it seemed, could be found for sale here: cloth, rice, tea, soy sauce, fine pottery—everything from precious jewelry to bamboo chopsticks. Osaka was all about business, and Seikei noticed that whenever someone in the passing crowd recognized Denzaburo, they hailed him with the question, "Are you making money?" That was the way Father and his business associates had always greeted each other, Seikei remembered. Now, it seemed, Denzaburo had truly taken Father's place.

They turned a corner and found themselves on

Dotombori—the wide avenue that always looked like a festival scene. Bright colored-paper lanterns were strung above the street, and dozens of banners with huge bold lettering on them hung from every building. Just as the people of Osaka liked to make money, so too did they enjoy themselves, spending their profits on pleasure and fun—and this was the place where they had the most fun.

Seikei had been in Yoshiwara, the pleasure quarter of Edo, but that had been a furtive place, hidden away from the main part of the city, where samurai disguised themselves before entering. Here, in Dotombori, the fun spilled out of the doors and onto the streets as people in front of each establishment beat drums, gongs, or bells to entice passersby to enter. Street performers—acrobats, jugglers, musicians—offered entertainment in return for coins. Seikei recalled the few occasions when Father had sent him to deliver tea here, and Seikei always lingered, just to gape at the scene, even though Father would later scold him for taking so long. Now, he reflected, he could spend as much time as he wished. The judge had even given him money to spend. The only thing to decide was where to go first.

Denzaburo, acting as if all the enticing scenes meant nothing to him, led Seikei to a building where the ban-

ner out front read NINGYO JORURI TAKEMOTO—the Takemoto Puppet Theater. An elderly man at the door took
money from Denzaburo and let them in.

Seikei saw at once that this was quite a different place
from the *kabuki* theater where he had once played a part
in order to capture the jewel thief Tomomi. The section
where the audience sat here was much smaller, and the
stage was divided into two sections, one for the puppets
and one for the narrator and musicians.

A show was already going on as they entered. Denzaburo had told Seikei that the plays were presented one
after another for most of the day and until people
stopped coming at night. They found three seats together close to the stage. Seikei sat between his brother
and sister, who told him what was going on. "It's a love-
suicide drama," Asako whispered. "They're very popular." Just as in the kabuki plays, thought Seikei.

The puppets, of course, did not speak. The entire
play was narrated by a man seated cross-legged on a platform to the left of the main stage. He had a powerful
voice that filled the theater. Suddenly a woman's voice
took its place. For a moment, Seikei wondered where
the female narrator was—until he realized that the
source was the same man. He not only told the story of
the play, but took all the speaking roles as well.

Next to him sat a samisen player, whose skill matched that of the narrator's. Though he had only one instrument, with three strings, he was able to enhance any dramatic situation, whether they were love scenes, moments of danger, or angry battles. Sometimes he played but a single note, but the plucked string made a sound that matched perfectly the emotion in his partner's voice.

At first Seikei could barely take his eyes off these two performers. But gradually their contribution became what it was supposed to be: only a part of the real show, the joruri. Seikei turned his full attention on the puppets. They were large—about two-thirds as big as real human beings. At first they appeared to be moving on their own, but as Seikei's eyes became accustomed to the light, he saw that larger shapes moved about the dolls—shapes covered entirely in black cloth. These were the puppet masters, those who gave the puppets their life and movement.

There seemed to be far more puppeteers than puppets. A low barrier at the front of the stage helped to conceal them, but several dark forms rose above it, and for each puppet there seemed to be one dark form that towered above the rest. "How many are there?" Seikei asked Asako.

"Three for each of the puppets," she told him.

Now that he knew, Seikei could pick them out. The one who was taller than the others controlled his puppet's head and right arm. A second puppeteer moved the left arm, and the third, who had to twist around swiftly to keep out of the way of the other two, made the legs move. Most of the time, he was hidden below the panel.

The two puppets on stage at the moment were a young man and woman. Dressed in bright clothing, they seemed far more real than the hooded figures who manipulated them. The story was a familiar one, but its appeal to audiences never seemed to wear thin. The young man was the son of a shopkeeper. He was deeply in love with the woman, who was the servant of a wealthy man. Her parents, in need of money, had sold her services to him for a period of years. If she left before her contract was fulfilled, her master could reclaim all the money from her parents, and they would starve.

Yet the two lovers' passion for each other could not be conquered. The young man had met his beloved in a forest, where he declared his feelings for her, begging her to stay with him—a completely impossible course, as they knew, as the audience knew. Did she not share his love? He pleaded for her to answer, to deny it if she could. Of course, she could not.

Sounds came from offstage. They sounded like hoof-beats. The shrill notes of the samisen created alarm and anxiety. The lovers were being pursued. They tried to flee, but suddenly a third figure appeared: the young woman's master, and indeed, Seikei saw, he was on horseback—a puppet horse manipulated as skillfully as the humans.

The newcomer dismounted, shouting angrily at the lovers. Rashly, the young man stepped forward and appealed to his generous spirit. Release the woman from her obligations, he pleaded. Allow her to marry.

This appeal met only mockery. The woman's master pointed out that the young man was not wealthy enough to afford a wife. His father would reject him if he married, and both he and his beloved would starve.

Stung by these words, particularly because they were true, the young man threw himself onto the woman's master. Their struggle was an impressive sight, as six puppeteers had to coordinate their movements while the samisen player strummed low notes of anger and violence. The third puppet, the young woman, put her hands to her face and screamed—or so it seemed, for it was the narrator doing the screaming.

The emotion of the scene swept everyone along with it. Seikei could sense the audience's sympathy for the young couple. He himself momentarily had the urge to stop the fight before remembering that it was only a play, just puppets fighting.

A gasp swept through the theater as a knife appeared onstage. The woman's master had drawn it from his garment, and the young man barely avoided being stabbed by ducking under the man's wild thrust.

From where Seikei sat, it looked like a real knife. He blinked, wondering how a puppet could hold and use it so skillfully. Before he could discover the secret, the young woman threw herself between the two men. Without thinking, the man wielding the knife thrust it into her body.

The music stopped. The narrator fell silent. The entire audience held its breath, and the young woman put her hand inside her *kimono* and slowly, slowly drew it out. Another gasp, and a single plucked string of the samisen accompanied her gesture as she lifted her hand to show that it was covered with blood.

She stumbled, fell to her knees, and let out a low moan. She looked up at the young man, her lover, and even though they were puppets, her longing gaze moved the audience more than words could have.

The man who had stabbed her, coward that he was,

threw his knife to the ground. "This is your fault," he snarled at the young man, and with that, he mounted his horse and rode off.

Kneeling beside his beloved, the young man held her tenderly. They pledged their unending love once more, and then she shut her eyes—really did shut her eyes, Seikei noticed—and gave up her spirit.

The young man hung his head to hide his tears, but everyone in the theater could hear him sobbing. The audience knew what he had to do, even before he announced that there was only one way for them to be together. The music grew louder, more insistent. The tension rose. The young man picked up the bloody knife and held it before his eyes, staring at his fate. With a bold stroke, he plunged it into his chest. Seikei could hear the sound of grunts all around him as people in the audience felt the blow.

With a last look at his beloved, the young man fell to the ground, drifting as easily as a falling cherry blossom in the late spring, and came to rest next to her. The last notes of the music echoed through the theater and then faded.

Someone drew a curtain softly across the stage. The platform that held the narrator and the samisen player slowly turned, and they disappeared from sight. Seikei saw that a screen divided the platform in two. The side that was empty now faced the audience.

People gradually relaxed. Some took out boxes of food that they had brought, and others began to chat. But no one left. Another performance would start soon.

"What did you think?" Asako asked.

"Very . . . lifelike," said Seikei. "But it's unusual to present a play about such people."

He could tell immediately that had been the wrong thing to say. "What do you mean, 'such people'?" Asako asked.

"Well," Seikei explained, "I just mean, people who are not . . . not . . ."

"Samurai?" Asako suggested. "Like you?"

"Not samurai exactly," said Seikei. "I wouldn't expect anyone to write a play about me. I meant it isn't usual to write about shopkeepers and servants."

"Perhaps not in Edo," Asako said coldly, "where everyone is a samurai. But here in Osaka, the greatest of all playwrights used shopkeepers and servants—and people who are not such high rank as yourself—as his characters."

"Who was that?" asked Seikei.

"Chikamatsu. He used to write plays for this very

theater. Of course, he himself was a samurai. I thought you would have heard of him."

Denzaburo leaned closer to Seikei. "Wait till the next play. That's the one people have come to see. It's about far worse people than shopkeepers. Asako is just defending the boy she wants to marry. *He* writes only love-suicide plays."

Asako bit her lip and looked away. Seikei felt her anger. "Did your . . . friend write the play we just saw?" he asked her.

She acted as if she hadn't heard, but Denzaburo replied for her. "Of course not. He's still an apprentice at the theater. That was probably him, the third puppeteer working the young woman. He was crawling on the floor most of the time."

"Ojoji is very talented," said Asako sharply. "They won't perform his plays because the other members of the troupe are jealous."

Denzaburo continued to explain the situation to Seikei. "He'll remain an apprentice for years. Apprentices earn barely anything, so he can't ask Asako to marry him. It's like a little tragic play in itself, don't you think?"

Seikei glanced at Asako. The look on her face frightened him. He had seen that look on a woman only once before—on the roof of a burning house when Suzu, the woman he had discovered was a mass murderer, was trying to kill him. He started to warn Denzaburo, but his brother nudged him and pointed toward the stage. The curtain was opening. The next play was about to begin.

The revolving platform that held the samisen player and the narrator began to turn. Seikei saw that the two people on it now were different from the ones who had performed the earlier play. The samisen player was very old, with a few strands of white hair falling loosely across his skull. The other man, the narrator, sat perfectly still, his head down as if he were deep in concentration.

The samisen player picked up his instrument, cradled it, and then gave a cry of surprise. High-pitched, his voice sounded like an angry bird's, and some in the audience laughed.

Seikei didn't. He sensed that something was wrong, something serious.

4 ~

A Swiftly Solved Case

*T*he samisen player reached out and grasped the arm of the narrator seated next to him. He spoke urgently into the other man's ear. From his gestures, Seikei assumed he must be saying that something was wrong with the samisen.

But the narrator only slumped forward a little more than he already was. Seikei thought it might be possible that the man was only meditating, but it seemed far more likely that he was . . . Seikei didn't like to think it, but he had seen dead bodies before.

He felt it was his duty to see if anything could be done to help the man. He stood up, stepped past Denzaburo, and walked toward the stage. Some of the audience, seeing the two swords that marked his status as a samurai, muttered among themselves. His footsteps were what alerted the samisen player: when the man looked up, Seikei saw from his clouded eyes that he was blind.

"Someone switched my samisen," the old man said, and, as an afterthought, "and Kamori won't wake up."

Seikei took the shoulder of the other man and propped him upright. Now he could see a cord tied tightly around the man's neck. When his head lolled backward, his face appeared, and Seikei almost let him fall. The eyes were popped out of their sockets, and his tongue stuck from his mouth as if he had tried desperately to suck in some air in his last moments.

Seikei set the body on its back and turned to face the audience. By now, everyone was staring at him. Obviously, he thought, they would obey his authority, even though he was young.

"There has been a crime committed here," he said in a voice that didn't seem quite loud enough. "You should all remain until the local magistrate arrives."

A chorus of murmurs followed, and then a man stood up—a large muscular man who had a dark beard and mustache, with long hair hanging down the back of his head. Seikei noticed that his *kosode,* or jacket, was bright red with green frogs embroidered on it. The bottom edge was curved, not straight as was customary. The man lifted up one side of his kosode to reveal a short sword tucked into his belt. Clearly, the gesture was meant as a warning to Seikei. Then the man turned to his companions, who were dressed as oddly as he was, and said, "Come on. Show's over. We'll come back another time for our play." They all—five of them, Seikei saw—rose and marched toward the exit. Just as they reached the door, the leader turned and said loudly to no one in particular, "The play is the same as before."

It seemed to be a signal. The rest of the audience, virtually in a panic, rushed to follow the five strange-looking men. Seikei realized he would be wasting his breath to try to stop them.

"What's wrong?" someone behind him asked. Seikei turned to see the narrator from the earlier performance. He looked anxious. "Who are you?" the man asked. "What did you do to Kamori?"

"Someone took my samisen," the blind old musician complained again.

Seikei sighed. "Is there another exit to the theater?" he asked.

"Yes, in the rear, but—"

"Lock it," Seikei said. "And send someone to bring the local magistrate. Kamori has been strangled. Take a look."

The other narrator didn't look for long. He seemed to turn a little green, and rushed off.

The samisen player reached out and found Seikei's

sleeve. "Did you say Kamori has been strangled?" the man asked. "He's dead, then?"

"Yes," said Seikei.

The old man nodded, as if absorbing the news. After a moment he said, "We have been partners for thirty-seven years." Tugging at Seikei's sleeve, he asked, "Are you in joruri?"

Seikei blinked. "No. I was just . . . in the audience."

"It takes years to learn how to synchronize the music and the words," the man said. He seemed to feel it was important for Seikei to understand. "There won't be time for me to find another partner now." Tears formed in his blind eyes. "I always assumed I would die first."

Seikei's brother and sister, who were the only remaining people in the front of the theater, walked up. "I think we'll be going too," said Denzaburo anxiously. "Why don't you come along, so we can take you to our new house?"

"You can't leave," said Seikei. "You were witnesses to a crime. The magistrate will want to question you." He was irritated that not even his own relatives accepted his authority.

"We didn't see anything," Denzaburo replied. "We would be of no help. It's wiser not to become involved."

"My father is a judge," said Seikei. "It is my duty to stay here."

"Well, he's not our father," said Denzaburo. "Come on, Asako. Let's go."

Asako had been looking at the dead man. She turned to Seikei. "That's a samisen string around his neck. A musician must have done it."

"It's possible," Seikei agreed.

"I've got to stay," Asako said. "I can point that out when the magistrate arrives."

Denzaburo glared at her. "No one will think your boyfriend did this."

Asako pursed her lips together. "I'm staying anyway."

Denzaburo hesitated, clearly torn between his desire to get away and his wish to take Asako along. His dilemma was solved when a samurai wearing the shogun's crest suddenly entered. By the way he carried himself, Seikei assumed he must be the local magistrate. Two assistants, also samurai, accompanied him, along with the man from the theater who had gone to fetch him.

"Who are you?" the magistrate asked, addressing Seikei as a fellow samurai.

"Ooka, Seikei," came the formal reply in which the

family name was given first. Seikei bowed to show his respect. "My father—"

"Is the famous Judge Ooka," finished the magistrate. "I had heard he is staying in the castle." He bowed briefly. "I am Judge Izumo." He glanced at the body. "May I ask why you decided to punish this unworthy member of an insignificant puppet theater?"

Seikei was taken aback. "I didn't kill him," he protested.

"You had every right to," the judge assured him, "if he insulted you in some way."

"Look," said Seikei. "He's been strangled with a samisen string. If I had wanted to kill him, wouldn't I have used a sword?"

Judge Izumo shrugged. "A sword would be swifter, true. But if you didn't want him to die swiftly . . ." He paused and gave Seikei a sideways glance. "So you're saying someone else killed him?"

"Yes, obviously." Seikei had the uneasy feeling that Judge Izumo had wanted Seikei to be the killer only so the case would already be settled.

The judge didn't extend his search for a suspect much further. Saying, "Well, very likely it was this man," he pointed to the blind samisen player. "He's got the samisen, is sitting right next to his quarry . . . What would be easier than to strangle him?"

"But his samisen still has three strings," Seikei pointed out.

"This isn't my samisen," complained the old man. Seikei wanted to tell him to be silent before he got himself in trouble.

"Hm. Three strings." Judge Izumo was thinking it over. "Very clever. I see you've learned from your father." He turned to his assistants. "Search the theater," he told them. "Find a samisen with two strings, and arrest the person who has it." The men went off at once, and the judge turned to Seikei with a satisfied smile. "Tell your father we're not so slow to catch on here in Osaka," he said.

Denzaburo motioned to get Seikei's attention. "Perhaps we should go now?"

"No," said Seikei. He had no confidence that Judge Izumo would find the killer—or at least the real killer. He decided to question the samisen player.

"How can you be so sure this isn't your samisen?" he asked, without adding the obvious: since you cannot see.

"Oh, over the years your samisen becomes like a wife to you," the man replied. "You know her even in the dark, or even"—he smiled—"if you cannot see her. The touch, the way she rests in your arms, the way her voice sounds . . ." He strummed the strings of the instrument he held. "Hear that? This is a stranger. Perhaps someone else could make music with her, but not me."

"Well, when did you last see . . . I mean . . ." Seikei fumbled for the right words. "When did you last have your own samisen?"

"I always have her."

"But not now," Seikei pointed out.

"Ah." The old man nodded. "Yes. I understand. When was she taken from me? I can only think it was while I was deep in meditation, preparing for the performance. You know I can see the music when I meditate, and I become unaware of anything else."

"So you were not even aware that your partner— Kamori is his name?—was strangled as he sat next to you?" Seikei was skeptical.

"Kamori does exercises to strengthen his throat before every performance," said the old man. "To many people it might sound strange, but I am used to it. If he made sounds, I would not have noticed."

"Did Kamori have any enemies?"

"Oh, yes," the old man said with a low whistle. "Many. He was very cruel to the apprentices. They expect to be treated that way, of course, but Kamori was dreadful. He would also argue with the puppeteers, very often. They accused him of narrating too swiftly. They had a hard time making the puppets move fast enough to keep up. He often changed the plays too, and that would cause no end of trouble. He would even criticize the other narrators. Behind their backs, which is bad enough, but sometimes even to their faces, which is intolerable, as you know. I didn't like him very much myself, but it was my fate to be his partner in the theater. I only wish that I had died first."

Judge Izumo, who had listened to all this, took Seikei aside. "I know your father's clever, but this case doesn't require any great deductive skills."

"It doesn't?" said Seikei. "But if the murdered man had many enemies—"

"Yes. Clearly this is the result of some quarrel. It's now been settled among themselves, you see. These theater types—they're very emotional. Likely to cut each other's throats at any time."

"But someone must be punished," Seikei said.

"If you insist. We'll arrest someone soon enough. Ah, look, here's our man now."

The judge's assistants emerged from backstage with a samisen that had only two strings and, held tightly between them, a miserable-looking young man.

Asako cried out when she saw him, "Ojoji!"

His eyes met hers, and Seikei saw from the look that

he was ashamed for her to see him this way, a prisoner. "I didn't know it was there," he cried. "I swear. I was only returning the doll's knife to the prop room."

"Found the two-stringed instrument," one of the assistants reported to Judge Izumo. "And this man right in the same room with it. No doubt trying to hide it. Room's full of toys and other kinds of objects they use in their plays." The way he described it made it sound as if the plays were crimes in themselves.

"Good enough for me," said Judge Izumo. "Bring him along. This case is wrapped up."

"I didn't do it!" Ojoji shouted. "I was onstage when Kamori was killed."

Judge Izumo gave Seikei a wink. "He'll sing another song after some hard questions have been put to him, if you catch my meaning. These young ones don't hold up when they're pressed. When this one loses a few fingernails, maybe a couple of teeth, he'll admit his guilt readily enough."

"But you don't have enough proof," said Seikei.

"A confession is all the proof we require here in Osaka," said the judge. "If I'm not mistaken, that's all they need in Edo too. Believe me, young man, sometimes the simplest methods are best."

He went off, motioning for his assistants to follow with the prisoner. Seikei could only watch helplessly.

Someone struck him from behind. He whirled, ready to fight, only to see that it was Asako. "This is your fault!" she shouted at him.

5 —

The Master of Heads

Asako had listened carefully to Seikei's conversation with the judge. She realized that if Seikei had said nothing, the judge would have arrested the blind samisen player for the murder. Ojoji would never have been suspected.

"But I feel certain Ojoji is *not* the murderer," Seikei told his sister.

"What difference does that make?" she replied. "He'll soon confess, if they torture him."

"Well, there's nothing we can do," Denzaburo broke in. "Let's go find something to eat, as we planned."

"Why are you so eager to leave?" Seikei asked. "Don't you want to help prove Ojoji is innocent?"

Denzaburo laughed. "If you want him to be free, just go to your new father and tell him to use his influence. That's the way things are done, as if you didn't know."

Seikei was offended. "My father is not corrupt," he said angrily. Denzaburo just shrugged.

But he had shown Seikei what he must do. "I will find proof that Ojoji is innocent, and then I will go to my father."

"You can't do that," Denzaburo argued.

Seikei ignored him. Two Buddhist monks, clad in orange robes, had arrived and were preparing to place the dead man's body into a large basket. "Wait!" he called. "I'd like to look at the cord around his neck."

The old samisen player, who had reclaimed his rightful instrument when the judge took Ojoji away, said, "Can you untie it? I'd like to . . ." He held out his beloved samisen, still missing a string.

"I don't know," said Seikei, feeling that to use the string to play music again would be too gruesome.

Indeed, one of the monks shook his head firmly. "Everything that touches him, even his clothing, must be burned," he told Seikei, "to purify the things that death has violently desecrated."

The old musician heard. "I'll have to replace all the strings then," he said. "Two old ones with one new one—that would mean trouble in the house."

The samisen string around the dead man's neck had

been pulled tight and then knotted, Seikei saw. It was a peculiar-looking knot. Whoever had done this had made sure his victim couldn't free himself. It probably hadn't taken long.

Seikei took his hand away and nodded to the monks to finish their work. He turned to find that Denzaburo had slipped out of the theater. "He had to get back to the shop," Asako explained. "But I . . . well, do you really think you can help Ojoji?"

"I will try," said Seikei. "Do you know your way around the theater?"

She nodded. "I have been here to meet Ojoji. He came to buy tea at the shop one day, and when I learned what he did, I was interested. He invited me to visit. Eventually we fell in love, but as I'm sure you heard Denzaburo say, he has no money and I have no dowry. Which . . . doesn't matter now that they will execute him." She looked at Seikei. "Denzaburo was right, you know. Asking your new father to intercede would be the best way."

"I'll think about it," Seikei told her. He had no intention of doing that, but he needed her help. They went backstage, where they found a group of puppeteers and narrators arguing. The man who had gone to find the magistrate saw Seikei and asked, "Have they taken the body away?"

"Yes," Seikei replied.

"Some of us think we should resume the performances as soon as possible."

"But out of respect for the dead man—" Seikei began.

"No one had any respect for Kamori," spoke up another man, who was wearing the black puppeteer's costume, but without the mask. He towered over the others, and when Seikei came closer, he saw why. The man, a chief puppeteer, wore tall clogs that enabled him to hold the puppet high enough for the audience to see. "His departure will cause us a lot of bother," the man went on, "not the least of which is the attention of the shogun's authorities. I say we should pull ourselves together and act as if nothing is wrong."

"Easy for you to say," another puppeteer piped up. "Kamori wasn't a narrator for any of the plays you perform. How will I put on *The Messenger from Hell*? I need a new narrator and probably a samisen player too, because old Tayo will be useless now."

"Well, I've lost Ojoji from my team," spoke up another man.

"He was only an apprentice," muttered someone.

Seikei tried to raise his voice above the quarreling. "Do you all think that Ojoji was the person who killed Kamori?"

They looked at him, taking in the fact that he was a samurai and a stranger. It seemed to put them on their guard. "Well, the magistrate took him away, didn't he?" someone said. "Who are we to question his judgment?"

"But suppose Ojoji is innocent?" Seikei persisted. "Wouldn't you want to find the real murderer?"

The group began to glance at one another uneasily, as if wondering whether there was a killer in their midst.

"What's it to you?" one of them asked Seikei.

Seikei caught his sister's eye. She put a finger to her lips, and he guessed she didn't want her relationship with Ojoji made public. So Seikei responded, "I'm a friend of Ojoji's."

This brought on more disbelieving stares. A lowly puppeteer apprentice could hardly have a samurai for a friend.

"Can someone show me the place where Ojoji was found with the samisen that was missing a string?" Seikei asked.

There was a moment's hesitation. No one knew if Seikei had the authority to ask such a question. Then the gray-haired man who had narrated the love-suicide play stepped forward. "My name is Takemoto," he said. Seikei recognized it from the banner out front. "I'll show you."

He nodded toward Asako and added, "But no women allowed back there."

She nodded at Seikei and said, "I'll wait for you out front."

Takemoto led Seikei up a short flight of stairs to the prop room, which resembled the bedroom of the most overprivileged child in the world, Seikei thought. It was filled with everything a puppet might need, if a puppet lived in the real world. He saw, just at first glance, umbrellas, swords, carts, clothing, sandals, jewelry, lanterns, bunches of paper flowers—all puppet size—and everything was a bit brighter and more colorful than real-life objects.

"The samisen wouldn't normally have been kept here, would it?" Seikei asked.

"No." Takemoto picked up a puppet-size samisen. "This is what we use for the dolls."

A small jacket caught Seikei's eye. It was bright red with green frogs embroidered on it, and the bottom edge was curved. Seikei tried to remember where he had seen one like it . . . and then it came to him.

"What is that kosode used for?" he asked.

"Oh, that's . . . that's for a play titled *The Five Men of Naniwa*. Special costumes are needed."

Seikei decided not to mention that he had seen a man in the audience wearing an identical kosode. The judge had once told him not to share too much information with anyone who might prove to be a criminal.

"Who could have entered this room to take the string from the old musician's samisen?" he asked.

"Anyone," said Takemoto.

"Anyone who worked in the theater," corrected Seikei.

Takemoto shrugged.

"Besides the puppeteers and the narrators and the musicians, who else works here?" Seikei asked.

"We have a head master."

"A head master? Aren't you the head of the theater?"

Takemoto smiled. "Yes. But he makes the heads, and takes care of them. You see, the puppets are assembled for each performance. The most important part is the head, for that tells the audience what the puppet's character is. Come, I'll show you."

He led Seikei to an adjacent room. As he slid back the door, Seikei saw that it was indeed filled with heads. The sight was overwhelming, and more than a bit creepy. Each head, and there were dozens, was placed upright on the end of a stick. Together, all staring at him, they made up a doll world, with a whole range of ages and characters. They included animals and even supernatural spirits. He saw the faces of a beautiful young woman, a heroic young man, many older people, some with kindly expressions and others fierce, and a few that gave off such an aura of evil that Seikei shrank back from their stares.

A short man, barely taller than the puppets themselves, stuck his own head up from the forest of faces. The sudden motion made it seem as if one of them had sprung to life, particularly since the man's face wore a smile that looked as ever-present as if it had been painted on.

"Nishi," said Takemoto, "this is a young samurai who wishes to explore our theater."

"Ah," the man said, rubbing his hands together. "Perhaps you'll join our troupe. We're short a narrator and an apprentice, I understand." He giggled—a high-pitched sound that made it clear that he was the best audience for his jokes.

"I'm sure he wouldn't be interested," Takemoto said.

"Oh?" Nishi responded, cocking his head to one side. "Didn't Chikamatsu begin as a samurai before he saw the light and began to write plays?"

His attitude annoyed Seikei. "I once played a role in a kabuki play," he told Nishi.

Nishi giggled. "Ah, and what role would you be suited for?" He picked up one of the heads and twirled it on its stick. "A gallant young hero like this one?" Pulling a string, he made the head wink at Seikei.

"Or maybe you'd wish to be a mighty warrior?" Nishi chose another head, one that wore a helmet with two horns that made it look like a fearsome animal.

Seikei looked around, amazed by the variety of faces collected here. Then he pointed to one that had a wispy beard and long, flowing hair like the man he'd seen earlier in the audience. "What about that one?" he asked.

"Ohh," Nishi said. "That's a very dangerous one. You'd better not play games with him." Suddenly Nishi brandished a sword. Seikei instinctively put his hand on the hilt of one of his own swords, till he saw that Nishi's was merely one meant for a doll to use. Making swishing noises in the air, Nishi waved the sword threateningly toward some of the other heads. Then, abruptly, he struck at the one Seikei had pointed out. Just as quickly, the head—or what seemed like the same head—came flying in Seikei's direction. He dodged it, and when it bounced on the floor, he saw that the neck was painted red, in a way that suggested the bloody stump that would be left if the head had been real.

Nishi giggled so uncontrollably that he nearly dropped the sword. "That's a little trick we use to frighten the audience," he said, "when it becomes necessary to dispatch a character. But this one"—he raised his hand, showing a second head, the one he had chopped off before tossing the "bloody" one at Seikei— "Captain Thunder, he does it for real." He pulled another string and the puppet head's eyebrows moved up and down, making it look even more menacing.

"And could Captain Thunder have killed Kamori?" Seikei asked.

This brought on a new round of giggles. "Oh, no," Nishi said. "He and Kamori were *close.*" He brought the Captain Thunder head nearer to his own and gave it a kiss.

"That's enough, Nishi," said Takemoto. "You've told our guest more than he wants to know."

Actually Seikei had many more questions, but Nishi seemed to get the point, and his head promptly disappeared among the others.

Takemoto slid open the door, gesturing for Seikei to leave. "Nishi is a wonderful head master," he said. "But his imagination often carries him away. You shouldn't pay—"

He stopped because one of the junior puppeteers was running toward them. "Takemoto!" he cried. "Come at once! Tayo and Are are fighting."

Takemoto shook his head. "Impossible," he muttered.

"Yes," said the other man. "Tayo accused Are of being the person who stole his samisen."

6

TOO MANY SUSPECTS

*S*eikei soon saw why Takemoto thought it was impossible for Tayo to be fighting with Are. Tayo was the blind old samisen player, and Are, though able to see, was if anything more ancient than his opponent. But fury had somehow given both men unexpected strength.

Are was trying to grab Tayo, but two black-clad puppeteers were holding him back. Tayo overcame his blindness by slapping about wildly, hoping to strike Are but unfortunately landing his blows on the heads of apprentices who were trying to calm him.

"Stop it! Both of you!" shouted Takemoto. His strong voice, which could strike fear or joy into a theater full of people, did have an effect, but not quite the one he desired. Both men now turned in his direction and began to accuse each other—of the same crime.

"He stole my samisen!" shouted the man Seikei assumed was Are.

"Liar!" responded Tayo. "It was you who stole my samisen."

"Be silent!" shouted Takemoto, who had no trouble drowning out the old men's cries. When silence fell over the room, he said, "Now will some person who is not insane tell me the cause of this chaos?"

One of the puppeteers who wore high clogs spoke up. "Are discovered that his samisen, which was missing, was the one on the platform next to Tayo."

"Which I certainly would never have taken," said Tayo. "Who could possibly play music with that shabby old thing? He thought I wouldn't notice if he substituted it for mine. Imagine! I may be blind, but I'm not deaf."

"That's a lie!" shot back Are. "My samisen has a far, far more beautiful tone than yours, and that is why you craved it. You've envied me for years."

They struggled to get at each other again, but the other troupe members kept them separated.

"All right," said Takemoto. "Now you," he said to Are, "have your samisen back, correct?"

"Yes, but it will have to be tuned carefully after being in the hands of that clumsy—"

"Enough," Takemoto said. "Take it, tune it, kiss it, do whatever you must, but leave now."

"Aren't we going to continue the performances?"

"Tomorrow. Everyone's too upset today. I don't want anyone else killed." Seikei thought that the remark was a little strange. The two old men could hardly have killed each other.

Takemoto took Tayo's arm. "You also have your samisen back."

"It will have to be restrung," muttered Tayo.

"Do you want someone to do it for you?"

Tayo recoiled in horror.

"Fine," said Takemoto. "Then go and restring it."

"There's hardly any point," complained Tayo, "since the narrator I worked with for thirty-seven years is dead."

Takemoto pulled Tayo closer. "You can prove your greatness by learning to work with another," he said in a low voice.

That seemed to raise Tayo's spirits. He went off with a lighter step. Seikei noticed that he made his way without help. He knew the theater well enough to get around it, even without sight.

"All right then," Takemoto said to the rest of the company. "Come back tomorrow and we'll pull ourselves together and put on a show."

They broke up into small groups, talking among

themselves. From his experience with the kabuki troupe, Seikei knew that their lives probably revolved around the theater and nothing else. They didn't want to go home.

Seikei approached Takemoto. "Can I ask you a few questions?"

"I respectfully suggest that this is not the best time to learn about the theater," Takemoto replied.

"Just tell me one thing," said Seikei. "If Ojoji was not the person who killed Kamori, then who would be the next most likely person to have done it?"

Takemoto chewed his lip as he looked at Seikei. Finally he said, "I am."

Seikei could not conceal his surprise, but he remembered something the judge had told him: "Some criminals know that they have done wrong, and are tormented by guilt. These are the ones who will confess their crime if you encourage them."

"Why do you say that?" Seikei asked in a friendly voice.

"Kamori was trying to take the theater away from me," Takemoto responded. "Everyone knew that. I founded it more than forty years ago, when Chikamatsu was still writing plays, but Kamori said time had passed me by. He wanted to persuade the others to force me to retire."

"But surely they would have been loyal to you," said Seikei.

"The theater is an uncertain business," replied Takemoto. "The plays Kamori presented to the public always drew larger crowds than the ones I favored. If you want to stay in business, you must sell tickets. And his plays seemed to appeal to all types of people—merchants as well as"—Takemoto searched for the right word—"lowlifes, hoodlums. Particularly that play *The Five Men of Naniwa.*"

"The one that was going to be presented today, when he was killed?"

"Yes."

"But if you murdered him," Seikei pointed out, "then that would prevent your most popular play from ever being performed again, because he was the narrator."

Takemoto was persistent. "No," he said. "We have a talented apprentice narrator who can take Kamori's place. But he will not be able to force me to give up control of the theater."

Seikei nodded. He felt foolish. Takemoto was explaining why he could be the killer, and Seikei, instead of urging him to confess, was trying to talk him out of it. Perhaps Takemoto was being unusually clever. Seikei would have liked to consult the judge, but it was better to gather as much information as he could first.

"The apprentice you mentioned," Seikei said. "Did he get along with Kamori?"

Takemoto laughed, a dry sound. "I would have thought that by now you would understand that no one 'got along' with Kamori. Certainly not the apprentices. He treated them miserably."

"Then why would they have sided with him if he tried to take control of the theater from you?"

Takemoto hesitated before answering, "A very simple reason. Because he could help them make money."

"What is the name of Kamori's apprentice?"

"Joko."

"Is he still here? Could I talk to him?"

Takemoto introduced Seikei to a young man barely older than Seikei himself. He seemed uneasy, which made Seikei immediately suspicious.

"I understand you will take Kamori's place now that he's dead," Seikei said.

"Only if the others wish me to," Joko said. "It's always a group decision." His voice was smooth and deep. Seikei could tell he had developed it through long practice.

"Kamori was cruel to you, true?" asked Seikei.

"He reprimanded me when I did not measure up to his high standards," said Joko. He pursed his lips. "That is why he was such an excellent person for me to learn from."

"But now you feel you've learned enough to take his place?"

Joko gave Seikei a sad look. "No one can take his place. We will all miss him."

This was frustrating. Joko acted like a professional mourner at a funeral, hired to weep and praise a person he had never known in life.

"What about his taste in plays?" Seikei asked. "Is *The Five Men of Naniwa* a favorite of yours too?"

For the first time, Seikei saw that he had disturbed Joko's composure. He hesitated before answering, "It is not up to me to decide which plays to perform."

"Who does decide?"

"Kamor—" he started to reply, but then realized Kamori would no longer be deciding anything. "I suppose it will be a group decision, as usual."

"Why is that play so popular?"

Joko looked carefully at Seikei, as if wondering what to tell him. "Do you know that story?" he asked. "About the five men?"

It seemed familiar, but Seikei couldn't place it. "Weren't they criminals?"

"They were executed, if that's what you mean," said Joko. He couldn't keep his hostility from showing.

Seikei was puzzled. "Why were they executed?"

"Because they saw that rich people were living like pigs and set out to do something about it."

Now Seikei remembered. "That's right," he said. "They were a gang of robbers. They were caught and executed for their crimes. And rightly so." It had happened right here. Naniwa was an old name for Osaka, and people in the city still told stories about the five legendary gang members.

"Yet people still cheer for them," Joko said defiantly.

"They do?" Seikei blinked.

"For they died nobly," said Joko.

Seikei wanted to argue, for he could not see how it was noble to be executed for petty crimes. At least in the earlier play he had seen, the young man, though only the son of a merchant, had chosen to kill himself. There was nobility in that. Seikei hoped that he himself would be prepared to commit *seppuku* rather than show cowardice or bring disgrace upon himself. But robbing people, as the "men of Naniwa" had, was itself a disgraceful action.

He had no time for such arguments, however. He had to go to the local magistrate and persuade him to spare

Ojoji—even though he had uncovered no new evidence. But there was one more question he had to ask: "Who do you think might have killed Kamori?"

Joko responded smoothly, "I have no idea. Everyone respected him."

Seikei frowned. This was the opposite of what everyone else had been telling him. "So you don't think Ojoji could have been the murderer?" he asked.

"I see no reason why he should have disliked Kamori," Joko said. "With Kamori in charge, our company would have prospered, and we would all have benefited."

"But," Seikei pointed out, "somebody wrapped the string around his neck. He didn't do it himself."

"Perhaps the answer was right before your eyes."

This was too subtle for Seikei. "I'm afraid you'll have to be more specific."

"It was the string from Tayo's samisen, wasn't it?"

"Yes."

"And who was right next to Kamori on the platform?"

The question hung in the air until Seikei responded. "Tayo is blind, a weak old man," he said.

"You saw him fighting before, didn't you?" said Joko. "Even though he can't see, he knew where Kamori was sitting. Perhaps he gave him a drug, or sensed when he was deep in meditation. Kamori always meditated before a performance to clear his mind."

Seikei shook his head. All his investigation had accomplished was to bring him back to the man he had vouched for in the first moments after Judge Izumo had arrived.

"I must go," he told Joko.

"Please return when the theater is open again," Joko responded with a formal bow. "We will do our best to put on a better performance."

There was something about him that Seikei just didn't like.

Asako was still waiting in the part of the theater where the audience sat. "Did you find out who killed the narrator?" she wanted to know.

"No," Seikei admitted.

"Well, you must suspect someone. Go to Judge Izumo and accuse one of the others."

"I can't make a false accusation," said Seikei.

"But Ojoji didn't do this. I know him well. He isn't a vicious person."

Seikei wanted to tell her that Judge Ooka believed any person could be provoked into a crime under the right circumstances.

Asako must have read his mind—something she had always been able to do. "That new father of yours—the judge—won't you ask him to free Ojoji?"

"I can't," Seikei said. "Not just yet."

"Everyone says he's very shrewd," said Asako. "That he

can identify a criminal just by hearing what the crime was."

"I have known him to do that," said Seikei. He recalled being sent on a long journey in pursuit of a killer, only to find the judge waiting for him at the end of it, knowing where the trail would lead Seikei.

"So," continued Asako, "why don't you just go to him and let him *solve* the murder?"

"I have to assemble all the facts before I can do that," said Seikei.

"No. You know what I think?"

Seikei didn't, but he was sure she would tell him.

She did. "I think you want to solve the case all by yourself so you can go back to your new father like a cat carrying a dead mouse and say, 'Look what I did.' "

Seikei smiled. "Asako, even if you're right, we have to go talk with Judge Izumo now."

The judge's headquarters were in a modest two-story building that had a banner out front with the shogun's crest. After Seikei identified himself to the samurai guards, he and Asako were ushered into a room where Judge Izumo was seated on a soft mat, drinking tea and studying a scroll. "Oh, it's you," he said when he saw

Seikei, who was getting used to the fact that nobody in Osaka seemed pleased when he showed up.

"I have nothing to report on the prisoner," the judge said before Seikei could ask.

"Is he . . . in good health?" asked Seikei.

"Was he in good health before?" responded the judge. Seikei looked at Asako, who nodded anxiously.

"I believe so," said Seikei.

"Then he still is, because we've done nothing to him."

Seikei nodded. That, at least, was good news.

"I know you're thinking we're not very efficient here in Osaka," the judge said. "But you can save yourself the bother of reporting that to your father. I already sent him a message describing your involvement in this case."

"Oh . . . you did." Seikei was a little worried about his father's reaction. "Did he reply?"

"Very courteously. He asked me to indulge your curiosity, for he has found that you sometimes display good sense."

Seikei was pleased. "So you thought I should be the one to question the prisoner?" he asked.

"Oh, not at all," said the judge. "You're much too lenient, I can tell. But the truth of the matter is that the torturer has taken the day off."

"And that's why you haven't—"

"Correct. Now, I know you will think I'm too lax an administrator, allowing my staff to come to work or not as they please. But the fact is I have some experience in these things."

He paused and looked at Seikei, who realized he was supposed to agree. "I'm sure you have."

The judge nodded emphatically. "And it's not necessarily a good idea to have a torturer who shows up every day." He gave Seikei a stern glance.

"Why not, you ask," said the judge, even though Seikei hadn't asked anything. "Well, because frankly when you have a torturer who is too enthusiastic about his work, he can sometimes kill the prisoner *before* he confesses." The judge spread his hands. "So then where does that leave you?"

"Um . . . not very well off, I'd think," said Seikei.

"Not at *all* well off," replied the judge. "About all you can do to solve the case then is go out and find some other suspect."

"To . . . question in the same case?" asked Seikei, who felt a bit confused.

"Naturally in the same case," replied the judge, with a look implying he didn't think Seikei was showing such good sense now. "That's the case you're trying to *solve*. And you can't bring it to a close without a confession."

"Unless you have some other kind of proof," Seikei suggested.

The judge shrugged. "Well, of course, of course. But no other kind of proof is as satisfactory as a confession. You can't go wrong with a confession. Take it from me."

Seikei nodded, trying to appear enthusiastic. "Perhaps, then, you will allow me to try to get the prisoner to confess."

"You?" The judge frowned, and Seikei sensed that Asako too was taken aback by this idea. He couldn't try to reassure her, however. Not in front of the judge.

"You don't appear to be experienced in torture," the judge said. "If you don't mind my saying so."

"I have other methods," Seikei said mysteriously (or so he hoped).

The judge shrugged. "I suppose it can't hurt. The torturer will be back tomorrow. Usually he only needs a day to pull himself together." He called a guard, who escorted Seikei and Asako to the jail, which was right next door.

"What are you doing?" Seikei's sister whispered angrily.

"You have to trust me," Seikei told her. "I need more information before I can free him."

"You heard the judge. He wants a confession. Ojoji can't withstand torture."

The guard blocked Asako from entering the jail. "Him only," he said, pointing to Seikei.

"Wait for me," Seikei told her.

She looked unhappy, but nodded.

The inside of the building was divided into small cells with stone walls. A few tiny windows up by the ceiling let in some light and air, but Seikei still found it hard to breathe. The guard took him to one of the few cells that seemed occupied. There, sitting on the stone floor, was Ojoji, looking miserable but unharmed. The guard said, "I'll be out front. Knock on the door when you're ready to leave."

Seikei tapped on the metal grating that was used as a cell door. Ojoji looked up. "Are you the torturer?" he asked.

"No," said Seikei. "I'm Asako's brother. I want to help you."

If he expected this to get him his first warm welcome in Osaka, he was disappointed. "Tell Asako I'm sorry," said Ojoji. "She should forget about me."

"I think she's seen too many love-suicide plays to do that," said Seikei.

"I'm not worth committing suicide over. I'm too stupid," replied Ojoji. "I should never have taken the samisen."

Seikei stared. "You did take it, then?"

"Yes. I was just trying to be helpful."

"But what . . . did you strangle Kamori too?"

"Certainly not," Ojoji replied. "What kind of person do you think I am?"

"Then what did you do with the third string?"

"I don't know what you're talking about."

Seikei was exasperated. "The samisen you were found with had a string missing."

"Oh, that was Tayo's samisen. I didn't take that. I noticed before the program that his samisen was not where it should have been—by his side. So, since there was little time to spare, I took Are's samisen and put it where Tayo could reach it."

Seikei nodded. "That clears that up. But didn't you realize Tayo would know it wasn't his?"

"Well, they say that," said Ojoji, "but he's blind, and isn't one samisen pretty much the same as another?"

"Evidently not." Seikei wondered how Ojoji could have spent time as an apprentice at the theater and learned so little.

"I only wanted to help."

"All right," said Seikei. "Now try to help me, and I'll see if I can save you."

"Nobody can save me," Ojoji mumbled miserably. Seikei fought down the urge to ask him what it was about him that could possibly have attracted Seikei's sister.

"What did you think of Kamori?" Seikei asked.

"I didn't kill him."

"But you didn't like him?"

"Nobody liked him. They were all either afraid of him or hated him."

"But Takemoto feared he would take over the company. How could he have done that if everybody hated him?"

"Well, he . . . gave people money."

"He did? What for?"

"To soothe their feelings. He was always changing the script, you see, and that made things difficult. The puppeteers had to change their routines, which meant more work. But the changes seemed to make the play more popular, so we were taking in money. And Kamori always seemed to have plenty of money to distribute."

"Just one play? He changed the script for just one play?"

"Our most popular play: *The Five Men of Naniwa*."

Seikei recognized the title. "What is it about that play that appeals to people?" he asked.

"It's about this gang of criminals who steal from rich people. The audience . . . There are people who want to be like them, dress like them. . . ." Ojoji paused.

"Act like them?" Seikei suggested.

"Maybe."

"Why would anyone want to dress and act like gang members? Why would a play make them do that?"

Ojoji waved his hand as if to say he didn't know.

"What kinds of changes did Kamori make in the script?" Seikei asked.

"He would change places where the gang went, the kinds of crimes they committed. Sometimes they robbed people. Lately they were smuggling things in by sea, so we had to build a boat for them."

"For the puppets?"

"Of course. And then some waves, wooden scenery. That meant more puppeteers onstage because someone had to make the waves go up and down. It was a mess, believe me. The prop manager complained so much about the extra work that Kamori had him fired."

"Maybe he killed Kamori in revenge."

"I doubt it. He got a job with another theater right

away. The only one who was upset was Nishi. The man who was fired was really Nishi's only friend."

"Nishi the head master?"

"Yes."

"He's a little strange."

Ojoji shook his head. "More than a little. He tried to take over the prop department after his friend was fired, but Kamori wouldn't let him. They got into an argument about the storage space."

"What about it?"

"It's on the upper floor. You have to enter by a staircase. I think it's in the prop room."

"What kinds of things are stored there?"

"I don't know. Costumes and old scenery, I suppose. The prop room has too many things in it already. Anyway, Nishi wanted to have access to the space, but Kamori put a lock on the door and wouldn't give anyone else the key. It was just a stupid argument. Nothing up there could be that important."

"So Nishi wouldn't have killed him because of that," Seikei said.

"You never know. One time, when one of the heads was damaged during a performance, Nishi tried to stab the puppeteer who had done it."

"Stab him?" Seikei wondered if Ojoji could be making

this up so that Seikei would suspect someone else. But Ojoji didn't seem that clever.

"Well," Ojoji admitted, "he only used a puppet sword, but it was sharp enough to have done damage if the other puppeteers hadn't restrained him."

"What about Kamori's apprentice, Joko? He told me he respected Kamori."

"I don't know if that's the right word. He feared Kamori."

"Why? Did Kamori beat him?"

"Occasionally. All apprentices are beaten just to remind them to pay attention."

"So why would Joko be particularly afraid?"

Ojoji licked his lips. He looked afraid himself, just trying to recall this part. "He knew more about what Kamori was doing with the gang members."

"The gang members who came to see *The Five Men of Naniwa?*"

Ojoji nodded.

"Are there only gang members in the audience?" It hadn't looked like that to Seikei when he was there.

"No, no. Merchants come too, sometimes even wealthy ones."

"It seems like an odd mix." Seikei wondered why even his own brother had wanted to see the play.

"Yes, but more unusual was that after the performance, Kamori would come out and talk with some of the people in the audience."

"The members of the theater company don't usually do that."

"He was the only one who did. And afterward . . ." Ojoji looked nervously about, as if someone else could hear them.

"Afterward?" Seikei prompted. "What happened then?"

"Then he would have the extra money that he shared with the rest of us."

8 —
NIGHT DELIVERIES

Seikei thought for a while. It would be difficult to un-ravel all the threads in this tangled case. Perhaps he should go to Osaka Castle to find the judge. But it was a huge place, and he was still a little in awe of it. He needed time.

An idea came to him. "Listen," he said to Ojoji. "The torturer will come for you tomorrow."

Ojoji looked sick and sank to the floor. "What sorts of things will he do?"

"I don't know," replied Seikei. He actually did know, but if he told Ojoji, it would be no comfort.

"I won't be able to resist," moaned Ojoji.

That was what Seikei wanted to hear. "Don't worry," he said. "I have a plan. You'll have to trust me."

Ojoji looked at him skeptically. "Are you really Asako's brother?"

"Yes."

"She's told me about you. You're better than Denzaburo."

Seikei was surprised and stammered out a reply.

"Anyway," Ojoji said, "I have no one else to help me. I must trust you."

"Good," Seikei said. "Now listen."

A short time later, Seikei strode into the magistrate's office. Unfortunately, Asako came with him, and he hadn't told her of his plan. It would be unpleasant, but more effective this way.

"Have you finished?" asked Judge Izumo.

"Yes," Seikei replied.

"Did you learn anything?" Judge Izumo obviously thought this was impossible.

"The prisoner confessed," Seikei said. He might have enjoyed the look of surprise on the judge's face if it had not been for the cry of dismay and rage that came from Asako.

"That's a lie!" she said. "He could never have confessed."

The judge gave her a sharp look. "Were you there?"

"No, but—"

"Then be silent."

Asako obeyed him, but gave Seikei a look that meant

76

she wouldn't remain silent after they were outside. He could feel the pent-up anger rising within her like steam inside a kettle with a tight lid.

"You will of course have to make a written report," the judge said to Seikei.

"I will see that you get it," Seikei said.

"Perhaps you'd like to do it now. I can have a scribe make a formal copy."

"I would be pleased to," Seikei replied, "but I have some business for my father that I must attend to."

"Not a problem," said the judge. "The executioner will not be here for another three days. We have succeeded so well in fighting crime that his services are required only once a week."

Seikei's knees felt a little shaky when the judge used the word *executioner*. But he hoped to find enough evidence to free Ojoji before the three days were up.

And if he couldn't? He gritted his teeth to ignore that thought, and instead tried to pay attention to what the judge was saying. He was inviting Seikei to bring his father to visit while they were in the city. Judge Izumo would like to share his ideas on criminal investigations.

"Certainly," Seikei said politely, bowing low as he backed toward the doorway.

Outside in the courtyard, Asako put a death grip on

his arm. The guard glanced at them, and Seikei was relieved he was standing by.

"How could you tell him that?" she hissed in Seikei's ear. The kettle was releasing plenty of steam now.

"I told Ojoji I was going to," Seikei said.

"You did? And what did he say?"

"He . . . agreed. He actually did confess. He admitted he moved the samisen."

"I'm afraid the judge didn't quite see that distinction," she said sarcastically. "So march right back in there and—"

"Asako, don't you understand? If I do that, he'll just have Ojoji tortured."

"Oh, now I understand," she said. "This way, he'll only be executed. That's so much better. You know, I thought you were smarter than Denzaburo. But he's only a—" Her face was red, but she controlled herself and kept from finishing the sentence. Even so, her eyes bored into Seikei's like a demon from a scary print. "You're just stupid!" And with that, she stalked off.

He thought of chasing after her, but decided it was better to allow her time to cool down. Besides, he didn't want to argue with her when the guard wasn't standing nearby.

He smelled something that reminded him he was

hungry. A street vendor was selling *okonomiyaki*—thick pancakes filled with a variety of tasty things and fried on a griddle. He offered a choice of vegetables, fish, octopus, or shrimp. Seikei chose one with fish. As he bit into it, the warm, salty flavor filled his mouth, bringing back memories. Seikei had not tasted his hometown's fish in two years.

"No fugu in this, is there?" he asked the vendor.

"No, no," the man said. "What do you think I am? A murderer?"

I wish you were, thought Seikei. It would make my task easier. I need to find a murderer to replace a man who already faces the executioner.

He ordered a second pancake, this one filled with octopus, and thought some more. One of his problems was that he had too many suspects. He hadn't even questioned all the people working for the theater, and he'd already found several who had reason to kill Kamori. Except . . . everyone seemed to agree that the troupe tolerated Kamori because he somehow obtained money that he shared with everyone else.

To discover the source of that money, Seikei felt he had to visit the theater again. Perhaps it would reopen tomorrow. But of course, Kamori would no longer be distributing money to anyone. Who benefited from that?

Perhaps the person who had been giving him the money in the first place? According to Ojoji it had been someone in the audience. Gang member? Why? Wealthy merchant? What for?

Too many questions. It was getting dark. Seikei would have to find a place to spend the night. He hadn't learned where his parents' new home was, and it seemed he would be unwelcome in his old one.

No matter. He had grown up here. He knew several monasteries in this part of the city where anyone could find a place to sleep and receive a hot meal in the morning as well. He walked slowly in the direction of one, trying to remember which bridge to cross to end up near the entrance.

Something bright caught his eye in the gathering darkness. It was the jacket of a man paddling a boat along the canal. The bright red color stood out in the twilight, and the embroidered green frogs seemed to glow even more brightly than they had in the theater. As Seikei slipped into the shadow of a building, he saw two more boats follow the first. Besides the friends of the first man, they each contained about a dozen barrels, of a kind Seikei recognized. They were used to transport tea.

His curiosity got the better of him. A trusting boatman had tied his craft securely to a post on the edge of the canal. Seikei loosened the knot and, silently promising to return it, stepped into it and pushed off with a pole. He had used boats many times as a boy, and the skill soon came back to him.

He didn't have to follow the others too closely. Seikei knew where all the smaller canals branched off, and only had to make sure that the three boats in front of him did not take one of them. Finally, he saw them take a left turn.

They had picked the canal Seikei was most familiar with. Not surprising, really, that three boats loaded with tea would choose this little canal, for there were several tea shops along here. But Seikei had a sinking feeling that they would stop at the one he knew best.

And so they did. Seikei moored his own boat far enough away so that he would not be noticed. The men in the three larger craft tied theirs to the dock under the sign KONOIKE EXCELLENT TEAS. At this time of night, all the other shops had shut their doors and windows tightly, but a light appeared in the doorway of the Konoike shop. Then it vanished for a moment before flashing again. This happened a second time, before the light was finally extinguished.

As if in response, the man in the lead boat raised a

lantern. Seikei realized it had a metal covering that could be opened and shut to expose the light. The boatman flashed his light three times before lowering it.

A figure came forward from the shop. Seikei could not see clearly, but it must be Denzaburo. The men in the boats began to unload barrels, setting them on their sides and rolling them toward the shop. It was clear that this was a shipment of tea, from the "new supplier" Denzaburo had mentioned. But why so late at night? Why the secrecy? And most important, Seikei thought, why were the men who brought it the strange-looking gang members he'd seen at the theater?

He knew better than to go down there and ask these questions. Instead, he waited to see what happened next. The gang did not unload all their cargo at Konoike's. After they completed their work, they moved down the canal. As Seikei followed, he saw the lantern signals repeated at a second shop, then a third. Finally the boats were empty, but instead of turning back, they followed a new route. Old memories awoke in Seikei's head as he recalled exploring the city years before. He realized that the gang had chosen a canal that would take them straight to the Aji River. The tide was going out now, and the current would in turn carry them down to the sea, unless they stopped along the way.

All very well for them, but if Seikei continued to follow, he would not be able to pole his own boat back upstream until morning, when the tide came back in. Regretfully, he watched the men disappear into the darkening mist, like goblins.

He went back the way he had come. As he passed the family tea shop, the doors were shut as tightly as those on any other building. All looked peaceful. But inside, he knew, there was a secret. He wondered if he should stop and confront Denzaburo, but there was more that Seikei needed to find out before he did that. When he questioned his brother, he did not want Denzaburo to be able to lie to him.

IT GETS IN YOUR BLOOD

One thing about sleeping in a monastery—the monks made sure you got up early. The sun was not even visible when Seikei finished a bowl of plain rice and a cup of black tea that the monastery provided for all its overnight guests. He thought of the much finer breakfast that the judge would enjoy—in another two hours or so—at the castle, but he didn't feel envious. The judge, at official residences, always ate with others and engaged in long talks about government business that Seikei found boring.

He left an offering for the monks and thought about what he should do next. Whatever the meaning of the strange boatmen he had witnessed last night, his first task was to clear Ojoji. To do that, he must return to the theater. But when he arrived, the front door was securely shut. He found an alley that led to the rear, where he remembered someone had said there was an exit. Sure enough, right in front of it stood Takemoto, the man who was, at least in name, the head of the theater. "Back to see us again?" he asked. "We're not open for business yet."

"Are you going to be?" Seikei asked him.

"I think so," he said. "Joko can take Kamori's place— or at least he thinks he can. Tayo will object, but he has to play the samisen with someone or retire. And where would he go if he retired?"

Seikei nodded. "And will you put on the play *The Five Men of Naniwa*?"

Takemoto gave Seikei a surprised look. "There's certainly a demand for it," he said. "But the third puppeteer for one of the major characters is now in jail."

"Ojoji?"

"Yes. We need someone to take his place."

"Don't you have other apprentices?"

"A few, but they don't want to take that particular part."

"Why not?"

Takemoto hesitated. "It's a difficult position."

"From what I saw," said Seikei, "all the third puppeteers do is work the legs."

"Essentially that's true, yes."

"So all he'd have to do would be to keep up with the others."

Takemoto smiled. "You catch on quickly. May I ask . . . Even though you are a samurai, you told Nishi you had theater experience. What kind?"

"I was with a kabuki troupe for a short time," Seikei declared, not wanting to tell the whole story.

"I knew it," Takemoto said. "You reminded me of Chikamatsu. He was a samurai, you know."

"So I've been told," Seikei replied.

"I know you've seen our little troupe under unfavorable circumstances, but . . ."

Seikei understood what the man was driving at, and it suited his own purposes to agree. "I don't know if I could be more than a temporary replacement," he said.

"Ah, it gets in your blood, my boy," Takemoto said. "It gets in your blood."

Seikei had to find a safe place to leave his swords. "Do you have any storage rooms?" he asked.

"Yes, they're—" Takemoto started to say, but then caught himself. "I'm afraid Kamori had the key."

"Doesn't anyone have it now?" Seikei asked, eager to get a look inside.

"Someone might," Takemoto admitted, "but the rooms are probably full. Let's go see if Nishi has a place for your swords." Seikei thought it strange that even the theater owner would not have a key. But he decided not to press the point.

The odd little head master was delighted to hear Seikei was joining the company. "Ah, yes, swords," he said, his eyes gleaming as brightly as the polished metal of Seikei's blades. "May I see?"

Seikei slipped them off his belt and reluctantly exposed part of one blade. "You're not supposed to take them completely out of the scabbard," he explained.

"Oh, no," Nishi said, shaking his head and smiling. "Because then you must use."

"They were a gift from my father's best friend," Seikei told Nishi.

"Of course," Nishi said, stifling a giggle. "Very precious. But here"—he gestured around the room, where dozens of heads still were displayed on the tops of rods—"there will be many eyes to watch over them." This time he couldn't control himself. He laughed uproariously at his own joke. The shrill sound made Seikei's skin feel as if ants were crawling over it, but it did seem as if the head room would be a safe place. The head master was always on duty.

Seikei's training began when the other two puppeteers on his team arrived. Sakusha, the head puppeteer, was an average-size man, but when he slipped into his high clogs, he towered over Seikei and the other puppeteer, a quiet man named Ooyu. Sakusha carried the main body of the puppet, and Ooyu attached the left arm, which would be his responsibility on stage. Ooyu had also brought the doll's clothing, which was, Seikei saw, almost an exact match (though puppet size) of the oddly cut red jacket Seikei had seen on the man who had delivered tea barrels to his family's shop last night.

Seeing the costume, Nishi went at once to a particular head, lifted it off its rod, and brought it over. Sakusha took it from him and carefully fitted it onto a rod within the puppet's body. Seikei recognized it. The head's loose hairstyle and facial hair, like the jacket, marked the puppet as the one Nishi had called Captain Thunder. "Is that—" he began to ask, when Sakusha struck him.

It was a complete surprise, and though the blow landed on Seikei's shoulder, it was delivered hard enough to stagger him. Instinctively he reached for his sword. Just as well, he thought later, that he wasn't wearing one. His temper might have caused him to do something rash.

"Apprentices do not speak unless they are addressed," Sakusha said in a stern voice. Seikei took a deep breath.

He silently hoped that his investigation would prove Sakusha was the killer. It would be a pleasure to turn him over to Judge Izumo for "questioning."

None of this was lost on Nishi, who looked at Seikei with a smirk that was particularly irritating. "Life of apprentice is hard, as you see," Nishi said. He patted the puppet's head. "You think you saw Captain Thunder somewhere else, maybe?"

Seikei merely nodded, wary of attracting another blow from Sakusha.

"People enjoy this play," said Nishi, "so much they want to pretend they came from it." Another giggle escaped from his mouth. It was clear he was full of them. "So," he went on, "if you dress like Captain Thunder, wear your hair like him too, maybe you'll be just as tough as he is, see?"

Seikei understood. He had heard the same thing from Ojoji. It was clear that Nishi could tell him more, but Sakusha cut in. "That's enough, Nishi," he said. "We've got to practice. Down on your knees."

It took a moment before Seikei realized the command was meant for him, not Nishi. A little too long, for suddenly Sakusha hit him again. The blow was not as hard as the first one, as if Sakusha realized he would be doing this often and needed to conserve his strength.

"That's where your position is," Ooyu explained, motioning for Seikei to get down on the floor.

Seikei did so, feeling wary now that Sakusha stood higher over him than ever.

Sakusha raised the puppet. "You see the legs?" he called down to Seikei.

"Yes." He would have to be blind not to, for they were dangling in front of him.

"You see the heel grips?"

On the back of each of the puppet's sandals were metal rings, which Seikei supposed were heel grips. "Yes."

"Put your fingers in the grips."

Seikei obeyed. "Now we walk," Sakusha said.

Easier said than done. It seemed harder than it had been for Seikei to learn to walk as a baby. Not only did he have to make the doll's legs appear to be walking, but he had to slide along the floor at the same time, wiggling like a fish to keep up with the other puppeteers. The two of them seemed to have no trouble knowing just when they were going to stop or change direction. But Seikei regularly tried to keep going one way while his partners were heading somewhere else. Sakusha tried to hit him twice more—fortunately, Seikei's skill at dodging blows was improving—and even attempted to kick him once. If the heavy clog had struck Seikei, it might have broken a rib, but he evaded that as well. Seikei began to understand why none of the other apprentices wanted to work on this puppeteer team.

Sakusha's fury only increased. "This is impossible!" he shouted regularly. "Isn't there another apprentice we can use?" he asked Ooyu. "The puppet has more brains than this one."

"We'll need him for the scene where the five men and the two samurai appear onstage at once," Ooyu said. "All the other apprentices will be working for other teams."

"Impossible, impossible," Sakusha muttered.

They kept practicing, and eventually Seikei learned to sense which way the others were about to move and how to keep from actually tripping anyone.

"It will be easier at the actual performance," Ooyu told Seikei during a break. "The music and the narrator will signal what we are about to do."

Overhearing, Sakusha shot back, "It will be worse! Joko will be narrating now that Kamori is gone, and who knows what changes he'll make in the play?"

They soon found out. Joko arrived and the puppeteers who were to perform the play assembled. It was quite a crowd. Even though some of the teams operated more than one puppet, there were twenty-four puppeteers in all. Seikei kept to the rear of the group, not wanting Joko to know he had joined the troupe.

As Joko outlined his changes in the script, people began to grumble and protest. Seikei could not quite understand why, for they seemed minor to him. The "five men of Naniwa" were criminals who seemed to have no real purpose in life except to taunt and steal from honest merchants and—surprisingly—even samurai. From what Seikei could understand, Joko merely changed the crimes they committed. In an earlier version of the play, apparently, the five criminals had smuggled tea into the port. That had allowed the puppeteers to stage a scene with boats—something they felt was popular with the audience. Now, in the new play, Joko planned to have the criminals steal silk, which they would use to impress their girlfriends.

"Girlfriends?" protested one of the puppeteers. "Before we had only one woman in the play. Now we'll need five. That's going to make us work double time, changing from one character to another."

"It has to be done," Joko insisted. "Some of our customers may bring their girlfriends to the play."

"Who cares?" someone else complained. "Why should

we change the play just to please a few cheap girls who aren't pretty enough to be *geishas*?"

Several people laughed, but Joko's voice rose above them: "In our play they will see themselves as geishas," he responded. "You all remember how Kamori rewarded us when the audience was pleased?"

Murmuring was the only response, but Seikei could tell they remembered. Still, it was strange they weren't more enthusiastic.

"We will continue to be rewarded if we please our friends," said Joko. "I can assure you, all will be the same as before."

That seemed to settle the argument. The puppeteers made sure they understood all the changes and then went off to practice. Seikei still had many questions, but no one to ask for the answers. Nishi stayed in his room of heads, and Seikei had to try, somehow, to please Sakusha.

10 —
THE BLEEDING HEAD

*S*eikei had worried that the most difficult thing about being a puppeteer would be the mask. From the audience where he first saw the play, it appeared that the outfit the puppeteers wore was a hood and a plain black gown that covered them from head to toe. It was hard enough learning to be part of the three-puppet team, he thought, without also being unable to see.

But as he learned when he first put the hood over his head, there were small slits in the cloth that allowed him to make out what was happening. Being on the floor for most of the performance, he couldn't see much, but at least he could stay out of the way so Sakusha wouldn't step on him with those high, heavy clogs.

If anyone was afraid to go to a play at a theater where a man had just been killed, it didn't show in the size of the audience. Seikei peeked out from behind the curtain to see that nearly all the seats were taken. The only empty ones were in the front row, which he thought would have filled up first. As he watched, however, the man with the red jacket and his four friends marched in and, acting as if they had every right to the best places, sat down.

No, thought Seikei, it hadn't been his imagination: the puppet known as Captain Thunder wore the same clothing as the leader of this real-life gang. The others with him also resembled puppets in the play they had come to see. Joko had said they might bring girlfriends, but they hadn't.

Someone smacked him on the back. Hard. It could only be Sakusha, and it was. "Dimwit!" he growled at Seikei. "What are you doing? Counting the house? They're not here to see you! Have you forgotten to get the props?"

Actually he had, even though it had been explained to him that when the action called for the puppet to use some object—a sword, a bag of coins, a lantern—it was Seikei's job to supply it from his place on the floor. Sakusha would make it appear as if the puppet had picked it up or taken it from his clothing. But it was Seikei who had to fetch them from the prop room before the play began. He took off in that direction.

He found Nishi, the head master, already there. "Aha," he said when Seikei appeared. "I was wondering who forgot to take the props for Captain Thunder. Just thinking about how much fun it would be when the captain is supposed to draw his sword, and Sakusha reaches down . . . and . . . ha! No sword!" Nishi found this hilarious, though Seikei cringed to imagine the punishment he would have gotten from Sakusha.

It reminded Seikei of the real swords he had entrusted to Nishi. "Are my swords—" he started to ask before Nishi interrupted.

"Yes, yes, precious swords in safe place. Not as safe as storeroom." His eyes widened mysteriously. "Got a lock on storeroom."

"What is in the storeroom?" Seikei asked.

"Ah, big mystery there. Better not look, eh?"

"Do you know where the key is?"

"Too many questions," said Nishi, for once not finding anything humorous in the discussion. "Take your props and go now."

"But—"

"Sakusha will be angry," Nishi reminded him in a singsong tone.

Seikei needed no further prompting. By the time he returned to the stage, the music was beginning. Sakusha gave him a look that resembled a volcano about to erupt, and Seikei quickly slipped on his robe and hood.

The three puppeteers took their places on stage, and the curtain rose. Captain Thunder swaggered about, Seikei managing to follow, while Joko the narrator explained how he had become an outlaw. He was the son of a pottery merchant in Osaka, but even as a boy he was always in trouble. The neighbors complained about him. His teachers gave him bad reports. Finally, when he began to steal small items from the local shops, his parents threw him out.

He fell in with a circle of young hoodlums like himself, and because he was the biggest and strongest, he soon became their leader. To show that he was his own man now, he took the name Captain Thunder. The other members of his gang had nicknames too: Chinese Dog, Three Worms, Chobei the Braggart, and Kohachi from Hell.

As each of these young men appeared on stage, the floor where Seikei was became more crowded. He kept bumping into other third-level puppeteers, who cursed him quietly and shoved him out of their way. That of course disrupted the action that the audience was watching, and Seikei was thankful that both of Sakusha's hands were occupied with the puppet Captain Thunder.

The audience didn't seem to mind the occasional lapses in puppeteering skill. To Seikei's surprise, they cheered for this gang of low criminals and every petty crime they carried out. Captain Thunder and his crew lived by their wits—stealing, cheating, bullying, and threatening others. Their targets, more often than not, were wealthy merchants. Sometimes the gang stole from their shops; occasionally they forced the merchants to pay them for protection. These scenes drew loud laughter from the audience. Seikei was amazed, for he knew from what he'd seen earlier that some members of the audience were prosperous merchants themselves.

Captain Thunder and his gang began to pursue women who were almost as disreputable as they were. These were women who dressed like geishas but had developed none of the artistic and musical skills of true geishas. Having once gone to work in a teahouse where geishas worked, Seikei knew the difference.

Nonetheless, one of these women was a person of pure heart, even though she had fallen into bad company. Named Maemi, she truly loved Captain Thunder and tried to persuade him to give up his criminal life. Refusing to take her advice, he and his gang stole a cargo of silk from a ship in the port and brought it up the Aji River. In the city, they sold it to merchants, the very same merchants they had victimized earlier. That drew knowing laughter from the audience, again showing how they enjoyed seeing the gang triumph.

When Captain Thunder presented a bolt of the finest silk to his girlfriend Maemi, she hesitated. Torn between her innate honesty and the temptation of luxury, she knew she should refuse the gift. But the captain played on her weakness: he told her that if she did not accept, he would give the silk to another young woman, her rival.

Maemi accepted the gift and went offstage. Another puppet, with a head identical to hers but dressed in a kimono made from the new silk, was in readiness and after a moment appeared onstage. To the audience, it seemed as if Maemi had donned Captain Thunder's gift and returned to be admired by him. But as she stood there, the samisen played a melody that was hauntingly sad. All eyes were on the beautiful puppet, and even from his place on the floor, Seikei could see tears running down her face.

It was a trick, of course, set off by the chief puppeteer working the young woman. It showed how skillful Nishi the head master was, for he had created a head that could shed tears. Seikei was surprised that Nishi himself was not in the wings to enjoy the hush that fell over the audience of shopkeepers and hoodlums as they watched Maemi cry.

Afterward, however, Captain Thunder grew too bold. The next part of the play never changed, apparently. In the following scene, the captain and his gang insulted two samurai, who unsheathed their swords, prepared to punish these ruffians. Captain Thunder was not awed. He drew his own sword (a prop that Seikei managed to hand up to Sakusha at the correct moment) and charged the samurai. His gang joined in, and at odds of five against two, they soon put the samurai to flight.

The audience cheered. Seikei's ears burned with indignation. He peeped over the top of the panel that stood at the edge of the stage, wanting to see who enjoyed seeing the samurai insulted—even if they were puppet samurai.

There, seated in the front row next to the five gang members—who of course were leading the cheers—sat Bunzo, the judge's most trusted assistant. Seikei recognized him even though he was dressed plainly, like a shopkeeper, and had left his swords elsewhere. Then Seikei's eyes drifted and he spotted something even more amazing: next to Bunzo in the shadows, also wearing the ordinary kimono of a shopkeeper, sat the man Seikei respected most in the world.

Just then, Sakusha stepped on Seikei's hand. Deliberately. The pain was so sharp he almost cried out. He had missed his cue and the puppet was attempting to run—difficult to do when his legs were not following.

Seikei scrambled to keep up. In the play, the forces of law and order had finally caught up to Captain Thunder and his friends. The shogun's officials had come to arrest them—and the officials were hard, tough men, like Bunzo. Captain Thunder knew that this time he had to flee rather than fight.

The three puppeteers managed to get the puppet offstage, and Seikei sat holding his hand, still throbbing from having been stepped on. "Blockhead!" Sakusha said, not screaming only because another scene was being played on the stage. "Did you fall asleep?" It was a good thing Sakusha's face was covered, because Seikei didn't want to see it.

"No, I . . . I . . ." Seikei could not reply that he had seen his father, Judge Ooka, in the audience, looking just as if he always attended puppet shows about gang members. Seikei feared that he had even seen the judge applaud when the two samurai ran away from Captain Thunder.

Sakusha ignored Seikei's babbling. "Two scenes from

now we must go back onstage," he said. "Where is the head?"

"The head?" Seikei looked at the puppet. Its head was right there.

"Not that head, you . . ." Sakusha took a deep breath and continued. "The head we'll need when Captain Thunder is executed. The one with the bloody neck that is displayed on a pole at the execution grounds, where Maemi steals it at the end of the play."

"Oh." Seikei had rehearsed the entire story, but no one had told him they were going to do the trick with the chopped-off head that Nishi had shown him earlier. "That head."

Sakusha gave a cry of despair and took a step toward Seikei. Fortunately the puppeteer's hands were both occupied with the puppet, for it looked as if he wanted to use Seikei's head as the one to toss across the stage.

"I'll get it," Seikei said, scrambling to his feet. He ran toward the head master's room. "It won't take me a moment."

Fortunately the backstage area was nearly empty, but as Seikei approached Nishi's room, the door slid open and someone else stepped out. It was another puppeteer, dressed in the same black outfit and mask that Seikei wore. The other puppeteer, seeing Seikei, put his hand to his lips—or where his lips would have been if he hadn't been wearing a mask over his head. Seikei supposed he meant they weren't to make noise while the play was going on. There was something oddly familiar about him, but Seikei didn't have time to think about that.

He rushed past the other puppeteer and into Nishi's room. Once again, he confronted the eerie sight of dozens of heads of all kinds—young, old, kind, selfish, good, evil—staring at him. "Nishi?" he said. The sound echoed around the room but got no reply. Perhaps Nishi was next door in the prop room. Seikei began to scan the heads, looking for the one with the bloody stump of a neck, the one he had to bring onstage soon.

Then he saw it. His knees buckled when he realized what it was. He wanted to run, but told himself a samurai does not fear death. He began to walk toward it. The head, larger than the others, had a bloody stump all right, but the blood was still fresh—dripping slowly down the stick that held it in the air. The eyes were open, but the smile was gone. Gone forever now. Nishi had met someone who didn't get the joke.

CASE CLOSED—ALMOST

*U*sed your sword this time, I see," said Judge Izumo. "What did he do to offend you?"

Seikei sighed. The worst thing about the murder—of course, not worse than it had been for Nishi—was that it had indeed been committed with one of Seikei's swords. Nishi hadn't found a safe place for them after all, Seikei thought bitterly.

"This is your sword?" Judge Izumo asked.

"Yes," Seikei admitted.

"I thought I recognized it," said the judge. "Beautiful blade. So you say you put it aside back here while you were playing puppeteer onstage?"

Seikei nodded weakly. He knew how that sounded.

"Doesn't seem right to me," said Judge Izumo. "A true samurai . . ."

Seikei put his hands over his face, only because it

would be too rude to put them over his ears. This was punishment even worse than the crime: to be lectured by Judge Izumo on the proper conduct of a samurai. If only Judge Ooka were here to advise Seikei what to do. But by the time Seikei had reported Nishi's murder and someone had gone to fetch Judge Izumo, the audience had cleared out, and Judge Ooka and Bunzo had gone too. Even now Seikei was wondering if he had really seen them, or if the mask had blurred his vision.

". . . so really, you should just admit that this strange fellow insulted you beyond endurance," Judge Izumo was saying. "No harm in that."

"He's dead," said Seikei. "You call that no harm?"

"You needn't be rude about it," said the judge. "Why did you come back here to the theater anyway?"

"I was trying to find out who killed Kamori."

"Ah. But you told me that young fellow in the jail confessed to that crime, didn't you?"

"Yes." Seikei knew that would come back to haunt him. Judge Ooka had once told him that when a person tells a lie, it stands out from the truth unless the liar is able to change enough of the truth to make the lie fit smoothly. And few people were that good at lying. "I . . . I didn't believe him," Seikei told Judge Izumo.

"Oh, I don't recall you mentioning that to me," said the judge, who seemed to be not quite as obtuse as Seikei had thought.

"It was just a . . . hunch I had," said Seikei. "And I came back here to test it."

"What did you find?" the judge asked.

Seikei wanted to tell him that the crime must have something to do with a play about five criminals who had been executed years ago. But that story was so bizarre, it would only make the judge think Seikei was insulting him.

"Perhaps you found out this fellow killed Kamori," suggested the judge, gesturing toward Nishi's head, which hadn't yet been moved. Seikei glanced at it, wishing it could still speak. "And then," the judge went on, "when you confronted him, he tried to grab your sword, and you were compelled to kill him."

Seikei shook his head. He knew the judge still wanted him to be the killer, but he couldn't lie about that. "I told you, there was a person in a black puppeteer's outfit who rushed out of this room just before I arrived."

The judge grunted. "A pity you couldn't identify him."

Seikei bit his lip. Having had time to think, he had an idea who that person might be. But he had no proof—

fortunately, for he feared it was a secret he could never reveal to the judge.

"You see," the judge continued, "our head master here . . . That's what they call him, isn't it? Too bad he couldn't keep his own head, eh?" The judge gave Seikei a sly glance. Seikei thought it was a shame that the only person who would find humor in the joke was Nishi.

When the judge decided Seikei wasn't going to laugh, he went on, acting a little offended: "Head master kills the narrator Kamori. Strangles him, do you recall? Where do we find the samisen he took the string from? Right in the next room, which this fellow the head master had access to. Then you come along, clever young samurai, son of Ooka, find the criminal, and are forced to kill him." The judge clapped his hands. "Case closed. Your sister's boyfriend goes free. You look good too. What's wrong with that?"

Judge Izumo would have made a good liar, thought Seikei. The story he told was quite believable, except of course that Seikei knew it wasn't true. Something about it bothered him, though. "How did you know Asako is my sister?" he asked.

"I made a few inquiries after I saw her with you yesterday," the judge responded with a smug look. "Tell your father we're not so slow here in Osaka."

"There's only one thing wrong with your analysis of the case," said Seikei.

"What's that?"

"It allows the real killer to go free."

The judge stiffened, and Seikei could tell he really was offended this time. "Well, as for that," the older man replied, "I spoke to some of the people who work in the theater, and they earnestly requested me to inform you that they desire you to keep away from here from now on. They want to preserve their own necks, you see."

Seikei felt as if the judge had struck him. "They think I killed Nishi?" he said, hardly able to believe it.

"That is the general opinion," the judge said dryly.

Seikei looked around the room, wondering what he must do. His eye fell on his sword, the long one, which was covered with blood that had nearly dried. "May I take this?" he asked.

"I think there is no doubt that it was used to kill the head master," said the judge. "So there's no need to investigate it further. You may take it."

As Seikei reattached his swords to his obi, Judge Izumo said, almost as if talking to himself, "You can put swords on a shopkeeper's son, but that doesn't make him a samurai."

With difficulty, Seikei forced himself to ignore the

remark. Others, he knew, thought Judge Ooka had been foolish to adopt a boy from a merchant's family. Merchants were at the bottom of the social class system— below those who made things such as pottery and paper, below farmers who grew the food everyone needed, and far below the samurai, who were at the top. Seikei's original father had often told him not to let that bother him, because they were wealthier than many samurai. But that had not prevented Seikei from studying the books that told of samurai ideals and admiring the deeds of great samurai. So he had been ready when Judge Ooka needed his help to solve the mystery of a stolen jewel. Since then, he had never given the judge cause to regret that he had adopted Seikei as his only son. He would not do so now.

He bowed formally to Judge Izumo and reached for the door. However, the judge raised a hand to keep him for a moment longer. "If I do not receive a confession from anyone else," the judge said, "the young man named Ojoji will keep his appointment with the executioner in two days."

"I understand," said Seikei. Either he had to find the killer or confess to the crime himself to save Ojoji.

He slid open the door to the head room. Someone evidently had been listening just on the other side, for

Seikei heard the person jump back. He looked and saw that it was Sakusha. Seikei was about to apologize to him for interrupting the performance with the news of a second murder, but he stopped when he saw the look on the head puppeteer's face. Sakusha, who only a short time before had struck Seikei for the slightest error, was now afraid of him.

Seikei paused and looked around. Several other members of the troupe who had gathered nearby quickly looked away so he wouldn't think they were staring at him. But they had been—and with the same expression that he'd seen on Sakusha's face.

They really did think he had killed Nishi. And, he realized with a flash of anger, probably thought he had strangled Kamori too. In some mysterious way, like a goblin, he had evidently been able to sit in the audience and go behind the curtain at the same time.

Takemoto was standing at the rear doorway, trying to smile but not doing a very good job of it. Seikei thought the man was encouraging him to leave. He needed no urging; he strode out and heard the door shut swiftly behind him.

Seikei took a deep breath. He had several things he wanted to do, but a proper sense of duty took him first to the nearest Buddhist temple. There, after leaving an offering, he handed an older monk the sword that had been defiled by killing Nishi. The monk slid it partway out of the scabbard and, seeing the blood, merely nodded. If he let his glance flicker over Seikei for a moment, it wasn't with a look of fear. "I will purify the sword," said the monk, "but you should also meditate here to clear your mind."

Seikei bowed and sat cross-legged on the floor. He focused on the smiling image of the Buddha, who had discovered the Four Noble Truths. Seikei knew the monk was right. Anger had been building in him ever since he had gotten over his first shock at finding Nishi. Seikei realized that as clever as he had thought himself, someone had shown their utter contempt by committing this second murder. Worse yet, he thought he knew—

He shook his head, for he was not yet ready to contemplate that thought.

Pride. He knew it was his outraged pride that was the source of his anger. The judge had once explained to him, "It is good to be proud of achievements, of right thinking and action, of the kind of person you are. But pride is dangerous. If you allow it to blind you to your own errors, to wrong thinking and wrong action, or to the fact that you are not as close to perfection as you had imagined, then pride will confuse you and finally anger you when your view of yourself is challenged."

Seikei saw himself in the second description. That was the person Judge Izumo saw, the shopkeeper's son who wore the swords of a samurai but was still a shopkeeper. There was no point in being angry at Judge Izumo. Even the members of the theater troupe regarded Seikei as a person who had used his swords unjustly and carelessly.

It was time to act. The monk returned with Seikei's sword secure in its scabbard. Seikei had no need to look at the blade. He knew it would be as clean and bright as the day it was first hammered on the sword maker's forge.

"I see you have tried to clear your mind," said the monk.

Seikei pressed his hands together and said, "I still have far to go."

"May your journey be a peaceful one."

It probably won't be, Seikei thought. But he knew where to go first. It was starting to get dark, but he was still able to persuade a boatman to take him down the little canal to the place where a sign read KONOIKE EXCELLENT TEAS. "They're closed," the boatman commented, as he saw the dark windows.

"Not to me," Seikei replied. He paid the fare and waited till the boat had gone. It was too early for another late "delivery," even if one had been scheduled. The doors of the shop were shut tight, and certainly had been locked from the inside. Seikei knew that if he knocked, no one would answer.

But he also remembered something Denzaburo had shown him when they were boys. Seikei's younger brother sometimes stayed out late, associating with friends their father disapproved of. To punish Denzaburo, Father would lock the door, thinking that he would change his ways if he had to sleep on the pavement. But Denzaburo got in anyway, and Father had blamed Seikei, thinking he had opened the door as a brotherly gesture.

Seikei had complained, and Denzaburo showed him the trick. The stones that lined the canal could easily be broken into thin pieces. One of these would fit into the narrow space between the door and the frame. Then it was possible to slide it upward to open the lock. Seikei had tried it once, just to see if he could do it.

The flat, layered stones were still there, and when Seikei rapped one sharply against the pavement, it shattered. Feeling strangely excited—for after all, he was only breaking into his own home—he slipped the thin

stone into the doorway. As he lifted it, he felt the lock resist and then give way with a barely audible click.

The door slid open quietly, and he stepped inside.
Almost at once he froze, for a flickering light appeared
just beyond the doorway at the other end of the room.
Asako entered, holding a small lantern that illuminated
her face. She gave a little cry as she saw Seikei standing
there, and raised her finger to her lips. Again.

12 –
THE MEANING OF THE PLAY

They stared at each other for a long moment. Finally Asako spoke. "What are you doing here?" she whispered.

"I came in search of the person who killed Nishi," he replied, somewhat more loudly.

"Lower your voice," she pleaded. "Denzaburo is asleep, but he wakes easily."

"Probably because he has to accept deliveries at the Hour of the Rat," said Seikei.

"How did you—" She stopped.

Seikei lifted the lid of one of the barrels—one that had not been here on his first visit. He licked his finger and dipped it into the tea leaves within. The taste was unfamiliar. "What is this?" he asked.

"We sell it to special customers as black tea from China," Asako answered. "Very fine quality and very scarce."

"And very expensive," Seikei added. "Costly because

of the high tax the shogun charges to allow it to be brought into the port. Only those who have his permission may import tea from China."

Asako smiled weakly. "Would you like me to fix you a cup?"

"I would like you to show me the documents that prove the tax has been paid on the tea."

"Oh, I'm just a woman," Asako said. "I know nothing of business. I'm sure Denzaburo could tell you, but he can't be wakened."

"You were always better at using the abacus than either Denzaburo or I," Seikei replied. "If you had been a boy—"

"Well, I wasn't, was I," she snapped, forgetting that she was supposed to be whispering. "So I just have to get by as well as I can."

"And how far will you go to do that?" Seikei shot back. All this was new to him. He decided he had spent fourteen years growing up in this house without learning anything about his brother or sister.

"What do you mean?" she asked.

"I saw you, Asako. When you were coming out of Nishi's room." He put his hand on the hilt of his sword, for he had no idea how she would react.

"You couldn't have," she said. "I was—" She stopped.

"Yes, you were dressed in a puppeteer's costume so that no one would know who you were. Where did you get it? From Ojoji?"

She stared at him as if he were a frog who had suddenly learned to talk. "I had no idea you were so clever," she said. "You and those poems you were always reading. Yes. Ojoji wore a hole in one of his outfits sliding around on the stage. I took it home to mend it."

"So the people at the theater . . ."

". . . thought I belonged there, yes."

"But why—" Seikei could hardly bring himself to ask the question.

"Why what?" his sister said. "I wanted to find something that would clear Ojoji. To prove he didn't murder Kamori."

Seikei felt confused. "And you found out Nishi was the murderer?"

Asako shrugged. "If that was you I passed in the corridor, you know that Nishi was dead when I got there."

He hesitated. "No, Asako, I don't know that at all."

She seemed not to understand for a moment, then put her hand over her mouth to stifle what was either a cry or a laugh. "Me?" she said finally. "You think I killed him?"

His silence was her answer.

"Seikei." She was whispering again, though the sound seemed to fill the room. "You think I am a murderer? Your sister? Don't you know me?"

He put his hand in the barrel of tea again and sifted some through his fingers. "Asako, I don't know who you are or what you have become."

She gestured toward the barrel. "That was Denzaburo's idea."

Seikei nodded. He could believe that. Denzaburo was always the one to cut corners, cheat a little, lie . . . Now he probably saw a way to make extra profits, and if that meant breaking the law . . .

"How does it work?" Seikei asked.

"What do you mean?"

"This whole mess . . . the smuggled tea, the gang, the theater, Captain Thunder . . ." It was sickening to think of his family involved in this. What would Father say if he knew?

"Does Father know?" Seikei blurted out.

"No. That's why Denzaburo encouraged them to move to a new house."

"What is the connection between this"—Seikei pointed to the tea—"and the theater?"

"I thought you knew. You're so clever," Asako said.

"Tell me anyway."

"People go to see the play *The Five Men of Naniwa*. At first, it was just a fad. Naniwa is the original name of Osaka, you know. The play is supposed to be about five people who actually lived. Then, after the play became popular, this gang appeared. They dressed like the characters in the play, took their names . . ."

"Who were they? Where did they come from?"

She shrugged. "Five nobodies who found they could attract attention. And they did. People like Denzaburo, who would never dress like that himself—wouldn't have the nerve—started to admire them."

Seikei couldn't understand this. "Why?"

"They were . . . different. It was as if they were saying they didn't care how other people acted or thought. They didn't want to be like everybody else."

Seikei nodded. He remembered what it was like, growing up in Osaka, where all everybody ever thought about was business, while he had the lonely dream of becoming a samurai. Several times, his father had reminded him of the old saying "The nail that sticks up gets hammered down." You were supposed to accept the role you were given in life and go along. Seikei hadn't.

But that was not the same, he told himself, as wanting to be a criminal. Just the opposite.

"They appealed to people who couldn't be like that themselves," Asako went on. "They started to borrow money from people."

"And people lent it?" Seikei was surprised. His father had always warned his children about the danger of lending money. It was one of the few financial lessons Seikei had absorbed.

"Little sums at first," Asako said. "They bought fancier clothing. Then they started to want more money. That was when someone came up with the idea."

Seikei nodded to encourage her. "What idea?"

"That they could do certain things, if they really didn't care about the law. Things that would help the merchants, who would share the profits, and everyone would benefit."

"Who thought up this idea?" Seikei wanted to know.

"Not Denzaburo," Asako said quickly. "He doesn't have that big an imagination."

"Could it have been someone from the theater?"

"Maybe. I'm not sure. Anyway, someone at the theater became part of the scheme. Because they used the play to signal each other."

"How did they do that?"

"At first, the gang just stole things from the ships in

the harbor. Whatever happened to be handy—bolts of silk, rice, writing brushes, anything."

"Tea?" suggested Seikei.

"Of course," Asako replied. "Anything that they could sell. If the goods were on ships in the port, then there must be someone in Osaka willing to buy—at a bargain price."

"And all the merchants knew of this?"

"All the ones who regularly attended plays did."

"How were the plays used to signal?"

"Whatever the thieves in the play stole, that was a signal to the merchants in the audience that it was available."

"So Kamori must have known," Seikei said.

"The narrator? Why?"

"Because he was the one who changed the plays. But . . . lately the changes were more extensive than that. What happened?"

"What always happens in Osaka," she said. "Everybody was so pleased they were making a little money that they wanted a *lot* of money. So the thieves were given a boat."

"A boat? Where did that come from?"

"Who knows? Maybe somebody stole it. Possibly they

bought it from a fisherman. Nobody tells me their plans. I'm just a girl, you know."

Seikei fought back the urge to say she knew an awful lot about dishonest activities—for a girl. "So what did they do with the boat?" he wanted to know.

"They said they used it to go to China."

"China?" Seikei was stunned. Japanese were forbidden to leave their home islands. They were told that China was a weak country across the sea, and that its ideas should not be permitted to infect Japan. Even so, some Chinese products, such as tea and silk, were highly regarded and brought high prices. A limited trade was carried on at the port of Nagasaki, where every year a few ships arrived from China and other strange-sounding places such as Holland. But any Japanese who traveled overseas without permission, which was rarely given, faced the death penalty if he tried to return.

"Isn't China very far away?" asked Seikei.

"Apparently not," his sister replied. "This gang was willing to go, and the merchants saw a chance for big profits. They put up the money to buy a cargo of goods in China, and Captain Thunder and his men set sail. Of course, some people thought they would never be seen again. Either they would run off with the boat and the money or else they would get into trouble." She shrugged. "Since he was *always* in trouble, that wouldn't have surprised me."

"*He* was?" Seikei caught something in what Asako had said. "Who was?"

"I meant they were, of course."

"No, you said 'he was.' Who were you talking about?"

She hesitated before answering, and Seikei knew he was right. "Asako," he asked, "do you know one of these people?"

"I knew him . . ." she said, "before he got into this gang nonsense. He wasn't a bad person, really, and I'm sure he isn't one now. His parents were cruel to him, so he left and fell in with some others who were . . . different."

"What's his name?"

"Well, he was just Kazu then, but now he calls himself Captain Thunder. Silly, don't you think?"

LOOKING FOR GOBLINS

Seikei was staggered. His own sister knew the head of a gang of thieves and smugglers. "But you . . ." he stammered. "What about Ojoji?"

"What about him?"

"I thought you wanted to marry him."

Asako nodded, but could not meet Seikei's eyes. "Unless he's executed," she said. "Have you found out who the killer is yet?"

"No, but . . . suppose it's this Captain Thunder? Your friend?"

"Don't be absurd. He's nothing like that."

"Do you love him?"

"What kind of question is that? How could I love him if I want to marry Ojoji?"

Vaguely, Seikei understood that Asako hadn't answered his question. But he was too uncomfortable to pursue the subject any further. He had never been able to win an argument with his sister.

"How can I find him?" Seikei asked.

"Who?"

"You know who. Captain Thunder, Kazu, whatever you want to call him."

"They have a place down by the grove of pine trees on the beach. But they won't be there now. Did you see the play tonight? Before it was stopped?"

"See it? I was in it."

"Well, it told everyone what kind of merchandise the gang would distribute next."

Seikei racked his brain, trying to recall the changes that had been made in the script. "Silk?" he asked. "They are going to bring silk here? And sell it to the silk merchants?"

"Easy when you know the secret, isn't it?" she asked.

"I must go there," he said, turning toward the door.

"Where are you going?" she asked.

"To Itachibori Street, where the silk merchants have their shops."

"They won't be there tonight. The signal was only to let Captain Thunder and his men know they should go pick up the silk."

"Where would they go?" Seikei asked, fearful that she would say China.

Instead she told him, "A village on the northern coast of the Inland Sea. The silk makers there are supposed to turn over to the local *daimyo* everything they produce, but Kazu, the captain, and his gang will give them more money."

"And then sell the silk to the merchants here in Osaka."

"Yes."

"That's a crime."

Asako shrugged. "If it makes everyone happy, why should it be a crime?"

Seikei had no answer. He wished the judge were here. *He* would know what to tell Asako. On second thought, Seikei was glad the judge wasn't here, to learn that his adopted son came from a family of criminals.

"Tell me how to find this place the gang uses as a hideout," he said.

"I already told you, they won't be there."

"I must go anyway. I have to . . ." He broke off as he tried to think. "There may be a clue that will tell me who killed Kamori. It might help me free Ojoji."

"It's a waste of your time."

"You don't know that."

She shrugged. "You know where the Hamadera pine grove is?"

"Yes, of course." Everyone in Osaka knew that, because one of the most beautiful views of the port could be seen from there. When Seikei and Asako were children, their family sometimes went there for a holiday, and their mother filled bento boxes with tasty snacks for them to eat. Somehow, the food always tasted better on the seashore.

"Farther down the beach from there is an old shrine. The priests who used to care for it either died or moved on. Kazu and his men took it over. A little inlet from the sea comes up almost to the shrine's entrance. It's a good spot for fishing, they say. And also for hiding their boat."

"I think I remember the place," said Seikei. "When we were young, Father told us to stay away because it was haunted by goblins."

"Kazu and his men have encouraged that rumor to frighten off people."

Seikei thought about the ghostly figures he had seen delivering tea on the canal the night before. "Yes, I can well understand why," he said.

Denzaburo had a small boat, and Seikei felt no guilt about taking it. Though it was night, the full moon overhead gave enough light to allow Seikei to navigate. As it rose higher in the sky, the silvery disc reflected off the water and beckoned Seikei toward the sea. Tsukiyomi, the brother of Amaterasu the sun goddess, was supposed to inhabit the moon, which appeared only after his sister had retired. Now was the time when Tsukiyomi reigned and mischievous spirits like him could roam free. All sensible people had closed their windows, locked their shutters, and gone to bed. The only ones to be seen on the streets were city watchmen, who would detain anyone who didn't have a good reason for being out.

Seikei knew that if he encountered any of the patrollers, he would probably be unable to convince them that he had to visit a shrine at the beach at this hour. So he tried to stay within the shadows near the banks of the canal, making as little noise as possible.

After he reached the Aji River, the current carried the boat. Though the river was wider than the canal, it was less likely that any patrolmen would notice him here. He tried to recall which direction the shrine was from the mouth of the river, deciding finally that it was off to his left.

As he approached the sea, the sight made him wish he had time to compose a poem. Here the moon's reflection was chopped into pieces by little waves that broke all along the sand. He beached the boat on the left bank of the river and dragged it onto dry land. When he turned to walk, he saw that he had guessed right: not far ahead of him, he could see the shrine. It appeared totally deserted, just dilapidated enough to suggest that the Shinto priests who once reverently tended it had abandoned the building. They would have for certain removed the sacred object—whatever form it might have taken—from the *honden* in the heart of the structure. Still, Seikei approached with a sense of awe and fear. It was said that wandering spirits sometimes made such empty places their homes—and spirits like those could be malign and dangerous.

He reminded himself that the gang members he was seeking might be dangerous too. But he saw no sign of the boat Asako said they had, and the stillness of the spot made him think they had gone somewhere else.

A high wall confronted him, and he circled around it until he found an entrance under a *torii* arch. The gate faced south, toward the sea. If there had once been a *shimenawa* rope across the entrance to ward off evil spirits, it had long ago disintegrated. Anyone—or anything— could enter, clean or unclean. Hesitantly, Seikei stepped through. He found himself in a courtyard that was covered with flat stones, some chipped or missing. Sea grass grew between the cracks.

Perhaps Asako had been mistaken. It looked as if no one had been here for a long time. No, Seikei told himself, that was just an excuse. He didn't *want* to enter the main building. The trouble was, whatever now inhabited the honden had no name. It might be worse than death.

Step by step he crossed the courtyard, approaching the wooden door that separated the honden from the rest of the structure. He mounted the three steps that led to it, and reached out. The door opened inward and he pushed it open, facing a yawning black cavity. He took a step inside, holding his arm out in front of him.

A hand—strong as any goblin's—suddenly grabbed his wrist. Seikei cried out and tried to reach for his sword. Unfortunately, his sword hand was the one now possessed by a goblin. Instantly, he recalled some advice Bunzo had given him during his training: never put your sword hand into an unknown situation first. Well, Seikei would not forget that again—if he lived.

He had practiced using his *katana*, the short sword, with his other hand, and tried to reach that. Before he could, another goblin captured that hand. The two of them—or perhaps it was a single goblin with supernatural strength—dragged him into the darkness. He tried to lunge back toward the moonlit courtyard, into the light, when something struck him on the head. Then there was no difference between darkness and light.

14 —
AT SEA WITH CAPTAIN THUNDER

Seikei felt himself rocking. It was as if he were a child again and his mother was holding him in her arms and rocking him to sleep.

But he didn't want to sleep. He wanted to wake up. Something hurt. It was his head. He would wake up and tell Mother, and she would make it all better.

No. He opened his eyes and saw the stars fading into a sky just beginning to become light. And now he heard the sound of waves. He was in a boat, and the waves were making it rock.

He sat up and immediately wished he hadn't, for it made his head hurt more. For a moment, he thought he would be sick, and closed his eyes.

"Hai!" a voice called, making Seikei's head feel like a temple gong that had just been struck. "Our samurai boy is awake."

The word *samurai* made Seikei reach for his swords,

but of course they were gone. He opened his eyes, more slowly this time, to see a young man with a stringy mustache peering at him. Not only was the man remarkably ugly, but he smelled like a fish that had been out of the water too long.

Seikei gingerly reached up and touched the back of his head. He found a lump that hurt when his fingers brushed it.

"Chinese Dog hit you a little harder than he needed to," the man said. "You gave us a scare, though."

Seikei stared at him. "I scared *you*?" he said, remembering how frightened he had been when he was grabbed.

"Well, not Captain Thunder, of course," said the man. "He's not afraid of nothin'." He winked. "Or at least he don't admit it, which is just as good."

"Is he here?"

"The captain? Oh, yes, we're all here. We sticks together."

"Where are we going?"

"Going? We're on our way to buy silk," the man said as if Seikei should have realized that.

"Is it far?" Seikei asked. If they were headed for China, then he could never get back in time to save Ojoji.

"We should be there before noon, unless we run into a storm. Then we'd have to lower the sail and wait till it blows over."

"Why . . . why did you bring me along?"

The man gave Seikei a look of disapproval. "Well, fact is, you forced us to."

Seikei touched the lump on his head again, even though he knew he shouldn't. "Um . . . how did I force you to? I don't remember that part."

"Well, you found our hiding place, didn't you? We couldn't just leave you there to wake up and tell someone about that, could we?"

"Ahhh, I guess not."

"O' course, we could've chopped off your head with one of them nice-looking swords of yours. Kohachi wanted to do that, you know. But that's just his way. 'S why we call him Kohachi from Hell."

Another character from the play, Seikei thought. Perhaps he was only dreaming and had written himself into the script. "What's *your* name?" he asked the man.

"Three Worms," came the response. The man sounded quite proud. "You know the story behind that?"

"You mean *The Five Men of Naniwa*?"

"Nah, that's just a . . . well, never mind. No. Recall

when you were a little boy? Didn't your mother keep you up all night on a *koshin* day?"

Koshin. Seikei remembered. It had something to do with the stars and what days were lucky or unlucky. His father said it didn't do any harm to pay attention to those things, unless it interfered with something you really wanted to do. Five or six times a year, there was a koshin day, and if you fell asleep that day, three worms in your body would escape and tell about your sins. Seikei wasn't sure who they told your sins *to,* but it wasn't supposed to be good. As Seikei recalled, he always got very tired and fell asleep anyway on koshin days. But nothing bad seemed to happen. Mother was the only one who worried.

Three Worms, whose fishy breath was uncomfortably close to Seikei, was eager to tell the story. "Well, they call me Three Worms because it's easy for me to stay up all night, see? I don't need much sleep. I'm the best person to put on watch." He winked. "I heard *you* comin' last night."

"You did."

"From a long way off. Fact is, I thought you must be three or four people. That's how much noise you made."

"I thought I was being quiet," Seikei muttered.

"What were you doing?" Three Worms asked. "Come to rob us?"

"Well, I . . ." Seikei wasn't sure what to say. It was disconcerting to have Three Worms accuse *him* of a crime.

"Three Worms!" someone behind Seikei bellowed, loud enough to make Three Worms jump. "Are you talking to the prisoner?"

"No, Captain, I never said a word," Three Worms said. He glanced at Seikei, as if appealing to him not to say otherwise.

The captain stepped around Three Worms and stood over Seikei, his arms folded. He wore the now-familiar red jacket, and up close Seikei could see that even though he was a young man, his face was pockmarked with the scars left by some disease. His wispy beard and mustache might have been unsuccessful attempts to hide those blemishes. He was also a lot bigger and heavier than Seikei had remembered. Just for a moment, Seikei wondered how or where his sister could have met this man, and what about him might have attracted her. Ojoji might have been a bit of a slow thinker, but at least he washed regularly.

"So what have you to say for yourself?" Captain Thunder shouted at Seikei. Like Susanoo, the thunder god, he seemed to think that the louder he was, the more impressive he became.

Seikei was offended that such a man would challenge him this way. "I am a samurai," he responded. "I don't have to account for myself to a thief and a smuggler."

Captain Thunder responded with a hearty laugh. "Bold!" he shouted, giving Three Worms a slap on the back that staggered him. "I like to see boldness."

He bent over to get a closer look at Seikei, who still sat slumped on the deck. "Haven't I seen you before?" Captain Thunder asked.

Seikei remained silent. "The theater," said the captain after a moment. "You were at the theater." When Seikei still didn't respond, the captain poked him with his finger. "Well?" he asked. "Weren't you?"

"Suppose I was?" Seikei asked.

"Arrrh," Captain Thunder responded, sounding disappointed. "What happened to that boldness?" He put his hands on his hips and did a mocking little dance. "Suppose I was? Suppose I was?" he chanted in a high voice.

He stopped, turned back to Seikei, and spoke in his normal thunderous tone. "Here's a question you ought to answer: Why shouldn't I pitch you overboard like a bag of puppies no one wants to feed?"

Seikei thought about it. He remembered what his sister had told him about Captain Thunder and replied,

"Then that would make you a murderer as well as a thief."

Seikei knew he was taking a chance. If Captain Thunder *had* been responsible for the murders at the puppet theater, then Seikei would have solved the crime. Unfortunately, he would probably also die as well.

A samurai does not fear death, Seikei told himself.

Then he saw Captain Thunder give him an amused look, and he knew that for now, he would not die. "If you travel with us, then," said the captain, "you'll have to earn your keep. No freeloaders in my crew."

Seikei nodded. He could have pointed out that he hadn't exactly volunteered to be a member of the crew, but there was no point in pushing things.

"What's your name?" asked Captain Thunder.

"Seikei," he said, since it seemed unnecessary to give his family name as he would have done normally. Captain Thunder might well have heard of Judge Ooka.

"Among us," said Captain Thunder, "your name will be Wooden Head." He looked at Three Worms, who laughed appreciatively. "Because that's what it sounded like when Chinese Dog hit you."

Seikei figured Wooden Head was no worse a name than Three Worms or Chinese Dog.

"Three Worms here will tell you what to do," said Captain Thunder. He went off toward the ship's cabin. Seikei gave Three Worms a questioning look.

"Not much to do right now, really," said Three Worms. "We only have one sail, and it's up. Captain steers the ship himself, so unless there's a storm, we won't have any work till we come into port. Maybe you'd like something to eat. We caught some fish earlier."

Seikei accepted a bowl of raw fish, a type he didn't recognize. Whatever it was, it smelled considerably fresher than Three Worms. "Are we going to China?" Seikei asked as he ate.

"China? What gave you that idea?"

"Oh . . . I heard you went there."

Three Worms gave Seikei a smile that revealed several gaps in his teeth. "Perhaps whoever told you that was listening to Chobei the Braggart. The merchants pay more for the things we bring them if we say they're from China."

"You've never been there? Even for tea?"

"We filled some barrels with tea we got in Tamano. Ordinary black tea. Maybe it came from China, maybe not. But Chinese Dog wrote some Chinese characters on the sides of the barrels. So when we sold it, people believed it came from China. Captain Thunder said nobody could tell the difference."

Seikei was annoyed. He should have been able to tell the difference when he tasted it in the family shop.

"This is a pretty good boat, though," Three Worms said. "We could sail to China in it if we wanted to."

"How far is China?" Seikei asked.

Three Worms shrugged. "Not very far."

Seikei could tell the man didn't have the slightest idea. "But you know," Seikei said, "the shogun's officials stop anyone who has left Japan from entering the ports. You can't come back, and if you do, the penalty is death."

Three Worms gave him a wink. "Who's to know? We'll just sneak in and out, the way we do now going back to Osaka. You're supposed to pay a tax for bringing goods into Osaka, wherever they're from, but we never do."

"That's a crime," said Seikei. He couldn't help himself.

But Three Worms didn't seem to mind. "Suppose it is?" he said, and Seikei realized that his own words had been turned back on him.

He finished eating the fish, but even though he'd been hungry, he didn't feel better. In fact, he suddenly realized, he felt a lot worse. He jumped up and headed for the railing of the ship. All the fish, plus some other things, went back to the sea.

When Seikei had finished, he turned to face Three

Worms, who didn't seem at all concerned. "What . . . what kind of fish was that?" Seikei asked.

Three Worms shook his head. "Just some fish we caught," he said.

"It . . . it wasn't fugu, was it?" asked Seikei.

"Fugu? No, you get that only in fancy restaurants where crazy rich people pay a fortune to eat it—and think they're lucky if they don't die."

"But I *did* get sick from it," said Seikei.

"Everyone does the first time they eat something in a boat," Three Worms told him. "It's better to get it over and done with. You can have some more now, if you like."

Seikei shook his head. He was still worried, even though getting sick had made him feel better. "But you said you didn't know what kind of fish it was. Maybe it really was fugu."

"We tried that once," Three Worms said thoughtfully. Seikei didn't know what he was talking about. "In the inlet where our hideout is, one day a lot of fish swam in and got trapped when the tide went out. We just waded in and pulled them out of the water in nets. Captain said we could get more for them if we told people they were fugu. But nobody believed us, so we gave the fish away, except for those we couldn't eat ourselves."

"You gave them away?" This was a strange gang of thieves, Seikei thought.

"Not to merchants," Three Worms said, correcting Seikei's mistake. "Just to some people who were hungry."

"But you could have sold them for *something*, even if they weren't fugu," said Seikei.

"Nah, the merchants who told us they weren't fugu would have just cheated us," said Three Worms.

"How could they have cheated you if you got them for nothing?" Seikei asked.

"The captain don't like to be cheated," Three Worms said firmly.

Seikei wondered if the captain had thought he was being cheated by Kamori at the theater. He was confused. The bump on his head throbbed, and his mouth was sour tasting. "Is there any tea?" he asked.

"See, you're feeling better already," said Three Worms. He went to get Seikei a cup of tea. Seikei looked around him. He could see a coastline in the distance. He wondered if the judge knew he was missing. If he did know, perhaps Bunzo would be looking for him. But how could he ever find me, Seikei thought, when I don't even know where I am myself?

15 —
THE SILK SELLER

*N*ot long after the sun rose, the boat drew closer to the shore. In the distance, nestled atop a twin-peaked hill, Seikei saw a magnificent white castle, with a central tower five stories high. The sunlight from the east illuminated one side of the castle and threw deep shadows on the other, making it appear like a great bird with folded wings.

"Is that Shirasagi Castle?" he asked Three Worms. Seikei had read about the structure, which was named for the egret that it resembled.

"To be sure," came the reply.

"And this is the city of Himeji? Are we stopping here?" Seikei thought that it might be possible for him to reach the castle, where he could find some of the local officials.

"We're stopping where the captain wants to stop," Three Worms responded. "But it's not likely. Too large a city, too many inspectors at the port. Captain likes to conduct business where money changes hands and off we go. We're bound for a place called Ako, if I'm not mistaken. But I never told you that," he added hastily.

He was right. Just after the sun reached its highest point, they came within sight of a smaller town, nestled on the northern coast of the sea. It too was dominated by a castle, though one far less grand than Shirasagi or the mighty fortress of Osaka. As the ship neared the port, Seikei could see banners on the castle, bearing the crest of a minor daimyo, one Seikei did not know. If he fled there for help, his story wouldn't be believed. As likely as not, the daimyo even looked the other way (for a cut of the profits) while illegal trading was carried on in the port.

Seikei's suspicions were reinforced when the boat landed. All along the dock people were streaming back and forth, carrying or carting barrels, baskets, bundles, and boxes loaded with goods. There didn't appear to be a single samurai to supervise the active trade, or to collect the shogun's tax.

Seikei went ashore with the gang members. Captain Thunder was apparently unconcerned that he might take the opportunity to escape. This was obviously a place where Seikei could find no refuge. Besides, the only way he had of getting back to Osaka was to stick with Captain Thunder and his men.

People were displaying their wares right out in the open here. Virtually anything seemed to be for sale—dried fish, barrels of sake, soy sauce, vases, paper, ink sticks, fruits, rice, and on and on. Each vendor—who might be only a single person, a whole family, or groups that looked as dishonest as the captain and his gang—called out the supposed virtues of their merchandise to the passing crowds. The tea, the vases, the soy sauce were all from China, if their sellers could be believed. The writing brushes were said to be made from the fur of monkeys that lived only on Mount Fuji. People hawked medicines, salves, potions, and charms that, they claimed, could cure any illness.

Seikei suspected, from what his sister had told him, that the gang was looking for silk. However, they walked right past several merchants offering bolts of silk, without even stopping to examine them.

A rickety two-wheeled handcart, filled with plums, came toward them. Pulling it, holding to the two traces in front of the cart, was a boy who looked about twelve. He seemed to be having trouble, for the cart was piled very high with its load of fruit. The boy was perspiring and breathing heavily, even though the weather was cool.

Walking alongside the cart, carrying a stick, was a man who might have been the boy's father, or perhaps only his employer. When the boy stopped to catch his breath, the man rapped him on the shoulder with the stick. Quickly the boy renewed his effort to pull the cart, and failed to see that a plank was missing from the deck in front of him. The boy avoided stepping into the hole, but unfortunately one of the cart wheels rolled right into it. With a loud crack of wood, the cart toppled over, spilling the fruit across the dock.

Enraged, the man began screaming and hitting the boy with his stick. The boy could do nothing but raise his arms to ward off the blows. A few passersby took advantage of the situation to pick up stray plums.

With a movement so swift that Seikei didn't even notice until Captain Thunder had gotten there, the gang chief seized hold of the man's arm. He twisted it, hard, so that the man gave a cry and dropped the stick. "Don't treat this boy like that," Captain Thunder said in a voice that, though not particularly loud, was full of menace. He gave the man a shove, sending him backward. He stepped on one of the plums, slipped, and fell to the dock. He sat there rubbing his arm, not looking as if he were going to give the captain a fight.

The boy appeared to be almost as fearful as the man.

He stared at Captain Thunder as if . . . yes, Seikei thought again how much the captain resembled a goblin who didn't have to follow the rules most people did.

"You don't have to take that, you know," Captain Thunder said.

The boy shook his head and muttered something Seikei could barely hear. It sounded like, "Yes, I do."

"You can come with us," Captain Thunder told him. Slowly the boy looked at Captain Thunder's gang, including Seikei. It was clear he didn't know who to be more afraid of—the man who hit him, or them.

"He's my father," the boy said. It sounded like an excuse.

"That doesn't matter," Captain Thunder replied. "It's time for you to make your own life." He gestured toward the members of his gang. "We go where we please, we take what we need, we do what we want. How does that sound to you?"

The boy's eyes widened, and Seikei realized what his answer would be. Captain Thunder's offer was too frightening for him to consider. "He's my father," the boy repeated, as if that was all he could think of to say.

Captain Thunder didn't argue further. He turned his back on the boy and walked on. The others followed, as did Seikei, who looked back to see the boy helping his father lift the cart upright. He wondered if the boy would ever think about the captain and regret turning him down.

Sometimes, Seikei thought, we have to make decisions before realizing how important they are. That was why he had wanted to become a samurai. He had read the books that described the code the samurai lived by. Whenever he had to make a decision, he had only to remind himself what the proper conduct of a samurai was—what a samurai was *supposed* to do.

Could he have lived like that if he had remained a merchant's son in Osaka? Or would he have been tempted to follow the path Denzaburo and Asako had taken? No way to tell. He *was* a samurai, and that gave him a way to live.

He hurried to catch up with the others, reminding himself that his duty was to bring Captain Thunder and his gang to justice, difficult as that seemed. Farther down the pier, Captain Thunder seemed to have found what he was looking for.

Five women, some young, some middle aged, were selling silk, displaying samples on bamboo racks. The sun intensified their colors and made the fabric shine. Seikei knew little about silk, but the quality of the material seemed obvious to him. The dyes the women had used were clearly of their own making, for Seikei had never seen such colors before. The first one he looked at was not only red, but had a touch of purple in it as well. Another was not pure green; quite a lot of golden yellow went into its unusual tint.

One of the five women, the youngest, seemed particularly pleased to see Captain Thunder. Though petite, she seemed unawed by his threatening size and fierce look. As Seikei came closer, he overheard them chatting about the need to keep secret where the silk came from.

The woman gave Seikei a brief glance. Though she did not stare, he felt as if she had noticed enough to make a judgment about him. She murmured something to Captain Thunder and he responded, "No, he won't tell. I'll make sure of it."

Hearing that gave Seikei an uneasy feeling, but Captain Thunder turned to him with what was intended to be a smile. "Do you know where this silk comes from?" he asked.

Seikei shook his head, half expecting to hear that it came from China.

But Captain Thunder said, "Maemi and her sisters and aunts make it in their village, back in the hills. It's hard work. They have to raise the silkworms by feeding them leaves. Not just any leaves, for the worms thrive only on mulberry leaves. Then Maemi and the others must wait until the silkworms make cocoons. The worms want to grow into moths, but before that happens, the women have to unravel the cocoons, careful not to break the fine thread. Show him your hands, Maemi."

The young woman fluttered a pair of hands that seemed as delicate as butterflies. "See how small they are?" Captain Thunder said. "You couldn't do that with your big clumsy hands that like to hold swords."

Seikei ignored the jibe, wondering why the captain was telling him this. "Then," he continued, "after they have unraveled thousands of cocoons, they weave it into silk. Again, a tedious, difficult job.

"But the work is not over," the captain said. "They gather berries and fruits and seashells and grind them up. From them, they make dyes with which to color the cloth. You like these colors?"

Seikei admitted honestly that he did.

"You know what is supposed to happen when all of that work is done?" asked the captain.

"No."

"Up in that castle," Captain Thunder said, gesturing without looking, "lives the daimyo who controls this territory."

Seikei nodded. The current shogun's ancestor, Tokugawa Ieyasu, had divided the land among the daimyos who had fought on his side in the battle to control the country. Their descendants still held the power and the land today. The farmers and craftspeople who lived in their domains were subject to their authority.

"So Maemi and her aunts and all the others are supposed to give part of what they produce to the daimyo. He sends his samurai to collect it."

Captain Thunder turned to the young woman and asked, "How much do they pay you for the silk they take, Maemi?"

"Nothing," she said simply.

"No? And what do I pay you for the silk you give me?" he asked.

"A fair price," she said. "Very fair. We could not live without the money you pay us."

"Does the daimyo know you sell your silk to me?"

She smiled and shook her head.

"Would you rather sell it to me or give it to him?"

Her smile grew broader. There was no need to answer.

Captain Thunder spoke to Seikei again. "When we go back to Osaka, I will tell the merchants that the silk came from China. They'll be glad to hear that because they can charge more for it. And their customers will proudly tell their friends that their kimonos are made from real Chinese silk. So. Will you say differently? Or do I have to kill you to silence you?"

Seikei's smile was not as broad as Maemi's, but it was clear there was only one sensible answer to Captain Thunder's question.

They stared at each other until Maemi interrupted. "I didn't know there would be six of you, Captain," she said. "I only have five special gifts."

Captain Thunder pounded Seikei on the back, a friendly gesture that Seikei realized he had to learn to endure (and survive) if he was going to travel with the captain. "Don't worry, Maemi, Wooden Head doesn't have a girlfriend."

Seikei wanted to ask how the captain knew that, and then decided it was better to remain silent. He wasn't sure why it mattered anyway, until Maemi opened another box and lifted out a gorgeous purple-red kimono, embroidered with cranes. There were, in fact, five of these kimonos, each a different color but with the same crane design. "For your girlfriends," said Maemi. "Lucky girls."

Now Seikei remembered. The five men of Naniwa in the play had five girlfriends. Joko had written them in to please the audience. Specifically, these five members of the audience. The most important members.

16 —
THE CAPTAIN'S OFFER

Seikei helped carry back to the boat the bolts of silk the gang had bought. By the time they had finished, he was hungry again. Being on dry land had cured his seasickness. The six of them went to a place that served fish and sake. Seikei drank tea, hoping to keep his mind clear, but each of the others downed several cups of the sake. Their talk grew louder as they celebrated what clearly was going to be a profitable trip.

Captain Thunder gave Seikei a look of appraisal. "Wooden Head, you heard what I said to that boy? The one whose father was beating him?"

"Yes."

"I make the same offer to you. Join us, and you can be your own man."

Or your man, thought Seikei. He had no wish to offend Captain Thunder, for it was clear that the man had a quick temper. Though he seemed benevolent now, his mood could change in a moment. "I have a duty to perform," Seikei told him.

"Oh?" Captain Thunder looked around the circle, inviting the others to share in the joke. "And what is that? To spy on us?"

Seikei frowned. "You brought me along against my will," he pointed out.

"But you came snooping around our home," retorted Captain Thunder. "What were you looking for?"

A deep breath. "I was trying to find the murderer of the two men at the Takemoto Puppet Theater."

Captain Thunder burst out laughing, and everyone else, except Seikei, followed suit. "Why would you think we had anything to do with that?" the captain asked. "If you know anything at all, you know that Kamori was our friend."

"I know he changed the play to tell the merchants in the audience what you would be steal—, er, selling to them."

Captain Thunder wagged a finger at Seikei. "It didn't always work that way. Sometimes the merchants had Kamori write in something to let us know what they wanted."

"And Kamori—" Seikei began.

"Was well paid for his trouble."

"But the other members of the troupe hated him," Seikei said.

"Who told you that?" replied the captain. "They loved him because he gave them all money. I told him it was wise to make sure everyone was happy. That's the way I like to do business."

"So who *would* have wanted to kill him?" asked Seikei.

"Perhaps someone who thought they should get paid a little more. There are plenty of greedy people in Osaka."

"If that was true, then who would want to kill Nishi?"

"Nishi?" said the captain. "Never heard of him. Joko's the one who became our contact after Kamori's death. Everyone wanted the operation to continue just as before."

"Everyone did?"

Captain Thunder nodded. "I told you. It's a business where we all profit." He put his face close to Seikei's. "So could you."

"Even Takemoto, the theater owner? Does he profit?"

"Of course. He couldn't operate the theater without the extra money."

Seikei was struggling to remember something he'd heard earlier. "Takemoto told me differently."

The captain shrugged. "He didn't want you to find out what was going on."

"Why not?"

"Because you're a samurai."

Seikei was surprised. "Is that all?"

"It's enough. Don't you work for Judge Izumo?"

"I never saw him before Kamori was killed."

"No? Are you a ronin? You look too prosperous for that."

"Not that, no," said Seikei.

Captain Thunder peered at Seikei, making him feel like a rabbit hoping to hide from a fox. "You came to the theater before anybody was killed," said the captain. "So finding a murderer wasn't your purpose."

"I only came to see the performance."

"Yes, but you came with someone, didn't you?"

Seikei hesitated, not wanting to reply.

"No use lying," said Captain Thunder. "I saw you."

The look on Seikei's face gave him away, and Captain Thunder nodded. "Yes, with a girl named Asako. Works in a tea business."

"She knows you," Seikei blurted out. Perhaps that was a mistake. He'd soon see.

Seikei thought he saw a softer look come into Captain Thunder's eyes for a moment. Then it was gone. Perhaps it had never been there. "Yes," he said. "She thought I should have become a merchant, a shop-keeper." The contempt in his voice showed what he thought of such occupations. "Instead," he went on, "I go where I please, I take what I need, I do what I want."

Seikei felt he had to respond. "I have a duty," he said.

Captain Thunder took another sip of sake. The foxy look was back on his face. "It seems to me," he said, "that I heard Asako has a brother. Not the slippery little character who thinks he's cheating me by paying a low price for Chinese tea. No, another brother—who could have been a shopkeeper too, but he ran off. Didn't *want* to be a merchant. That wasn't good enough for him."

Seikei felt his face burning, and knew that Captain Thunder saw it.

"So this brother," the captain went on, "became a samurai. Somehow I never heard just how he managed to do that." He cocked his head, waiting for Seikei to say something.

"Proved himself worthy, I imagine," said Seikei.

"Worthy," repeated Captain Thunder. He rolled it around his tongue like a piece of candy and said it once more. Clearly he liked the word. "And now, do you suppose that brother would like to take another step forward? To something better than a samurai?"

Seikei almost laughed, he was so startled. Better than a samurai? Joining this band of swindlers?

Captain Thunder was good at reading faces. "Have you ever seen China?" he asked.

Seikei shook his head.

"I have," said the captain. "And Korea too," he added, naming another of those places that people knew about only by rumor.

"It is forbidden for anyone to leave Japan without permission from the shogun," said Seikei. "Those who go are not allowed to return."

"I do many things that are not permitted by the shogun," replied Captain Thunder. "I . . . and my men. All you have to do is be daring. Daring enough to say, No man will tell me what to do."

Seikei was fascinated, but wondered if Captain Thunder had really been to China. He was skilled at bilking others, and because no one Seikei knew had ever been to China, Captain Thunder could say anything he liked. Who could tell if it was the truth or not?

Seikei remembered something Judge Ooka had once said. He repeated it now: "Those who act according to the laws," he told the captain, "enjoy the respect and support of their neighbors. Those who break the law live in fear of being caught."

"Pretty words," taunted Captain Thunder. "When you were at the theater, were you asleep? Or did you see how the audience applauded the so-called criminals on stage?"

Seikei admitted that he had. "But why?" he asked, wishing the captain could explain it.

"Because they admire us," the captain replied. Seeing Seikei's surprise, he laughed. "Yes, those greedy, conniving little merchants—oh, and wealthy ones too—they wish they had the courage to live the way we do. They would like to taunt and defy samurai too. For the samurai take money from the merchants in taxes and tribute just because they claim the right to rule us."

"The shogun protects us," said Seikei. "His samurai preserve order."

"Protects us from what?" interrupted the captain. "The only people I need protection from are samurai." He glared at Seikei, who unfortunately was the only samurai in the shop.

The gang member known as Chinese Dog, who never spoke when Seikei was present, leaned over and whispered something to Captain Thunder, who looked at Seikei and smiled. It was not a friendly smile. "Chinese Dog is tired of listening," Captain Thunder said. "He wants to try your swords—on you. But I offer you the choice of staying here. We must leave now if we're to deliver the silk that our friends in Osaka are expecting. And we cannot take anyone whose loyalty is in question."

It took only a moment for Seikei to make his decision. He had to get back to Osaka by tomorrow, for that was when Judge Izumo planned to have Ojoji executed. "I will not betray you," Seikei told Captain Thunder. "You have my word of honor."

"The word of a samurai, eh?" Captain Thunder responded. "I wonder how reliable I will find that." He looked around at the others. "No one has any objections?" he asked.

"He might be useful," suggested Three Worms.

"You're getting soft, Three Worms," replied the captain.

The return journey was not an easy one. Captain Thunder's gang liked to travel at night, to lessen the chances of encountering one of the shogun's patrol vessels. However, a storm blew up, making it necessary for them to lay anchor and wait. They couldn't see the stars to navigate, and they feared the winds might blow their craft onto the reefs close to shore.

The incessant rain kept Seikei from sleeping, and the rocking of the boat made him feel as if he would be sick again. He spent his time trying to think of what he should do once they returned. Would Captain Thunder really allow him to go free? And even if he did, how could Seikei rescue Ojoji from the executioner? Perhaps Seikei should just confess, as Judge Izumo wanted him to. The judge had indicated he wouldn't punish him. So everyone would be happy.

The trouble was, that was the way Captain Thunder thought—and for that matter, Seikei's sister as well. Breaking the law was fine as long as people benefited from it. Confessing to a murder he hadn't committed (or murders, for why not wrap up both cases?) would satisfy all concerned.

Including the murderer, who would go free.

Seikei also fretted about his promise not to betray Captain Thunder. Suppose the captain or one of his men had actually been the killer? Seikei felt he had read the captain's character correctly, however. The man was an arrogant scoundrel with no respect for the law. But he didn't seem like a murderer. Besides, he had been in the audience when both murders were committed, as far as Seikei could tell.

If not him, then who? With that question on his mind, Seikei fell asleep at last. He had a terrible dream in which a gang of puppets, holding their heads high on sticks, were chasing him. Seikei reached for his swords to defend himself, but they were missing.

He opened his eyes. The sun had come up, and the boat was under way again. As he stood up he saw that the sail had been raised and was puffed out in the face of a strong wind.

"Yonder!" someone called. The cry had come from Chobei, who had climbed atop the mast as a lookout. Seikei looked in the direction he was pointing. Another ship was off in the distance, a larger vessel with two sails. Seikei could just make out the hollyhock emblem on them, identifying it as the shogun's.

Captain Thunder adjusted his course to take full advantage of the wind. But the other vessel followed, and because it was swifter, the distance between the two craft began to lessen. Seikei saw men on the deck of the other boat, armed with swords and bows. Captain Thunder defiantly shook a fist at them. If Captain Thunder's men resisted, Seikei wondered, would the samurai slaughter everyone on board without asking who they were?

As the shogun's boat drew ever nearer, Seikei thought he saw a familiar figure. He jumped on top of the rail to see better. "Bunzo!" he called.

Captain Thunder noticed. He sent Chinese Dog to

drag Seikei over to him. "You know someone on that boat?" he asked. "Tell me quickly. I can still kill you."

"Yes, I know him," Seikei said. "If you surrender, I will ask him to spare your lives."

Captain Thunder spat on the deck. "What good is a life spent like a caged chicken?" he asked. He turned to Chinese Dog. "Get his swords."

They were stored in a chest on deck, and Chinese Dog soon returned. "Give them to him," Captain Thunder told his henchman. Chinese Dog looked as if he wanted to protest, but he silently followed orders.

"Strap them on," the captain told Seikei. "Look like a samurai." As Seikei attached the swords to his obi, he wondered if he should try to use them, even though the odds were still five against one. Captain Thunder thought of that, and grasped Seikei's right arm tightly. He motioned for Chinese Dog to take the other, and the two of them dragged Seikei to the rail.

"Stand up there," the captain said, boosting Seikei up. "Wave to them," he said, releasing Seikei's arm.

Seikei did so, and as he watched, Bunzo waved back. It was all Captain Thunder needed to see. With a mighty shove, he sent Seikei flying into the water.

You shouldn't have stopped for me," Seikei told Bunzo. He was wearing a fresh, dry kosode, and Bunzo was helping him clean his swords. Still, the sea breeze made him shiver. "You should have pursued Captain Thunder and his gang."

"Certainly that would have been the intelligent thing to do," said Bunzo. "For in the true order of the universe, you are an insignificant speck, not worth a moment's consideration."

You can always rely on Bunzo for an encouraging word, thought Seikei.

"However, as I am sworn to serve Judge Ooka," Bunzo went on, "I considered it my obligation to rescue you. For some reason, he places a value on your existence, and would have been displeased had I left you to drown."

"Even so, I'm grateful."

"Perhaps you can show your gratitude and prove you

have some use by telling me what you were doing on that boat and where it was going."

Seikei hesitated. He certainly didn't want to anger Bunzo, but he felt he had to keep his promise not to betray Captain Thunder. "Actually," he said, "I was trying to find a killer."

Bunzo closed his eyes. Seikei knew he did that to calm himself. This was not the first time Bunzo had been required to save Seikei in pursuit of a murderer.

"Who was the person who was killed?" Bunzo asked.

"In fact, there were two," Seikei told him. "They were both members of the Takemoto Puppet Theater."

Bunzo's eyes popped open.

"I saw you and the judge in the audience there," Seikei said. He felt a little pleased, because it wasn't easy to surprise Bunzo.

"Where were you?" Bunzo asked suspiciously. "Certainly not in the audience, or I would have seen you. You wouldn't have been able to disguise yourself that well."

"I was on the stage," Seikei said. "I was one of the puppeteers."

"Of course," said Bunzo. "You like to get into the middle of things. And I couldn't have recognized you because of the mask." Bunzo seemed relieved that Seikei had hidden himself only by using a trick. "But why were you there in the first place? Because of the murder of the narrator named Kamori the night before?"

"Yes. How did you know?"

"The judge had wanted to talk to Kamori," Bunzo explained. "He suspected that the smugglers we were investigating used Kamori to help dispose of their illegal merchandise."

"More than that," said Seikei.

"What do you mean?" asked Bunzo. "What have you learned?"

Seikei decided he wouldn't be breaking his promise if he told Bunzo about the messages given in the play. He had to be careful, though, not to reveal that he had learned it from his sister. Perhaps it was still possible to keep her out of trouble. Then he reminded himself that as far as he knew, she might still be the murderer he was seeking.

Bunzo nodded as the story unfolded. "We became suspicious of the oddly dressed gang," he told Seikei. "They have a bad reputation. But after the performance ended so abruptly, we weren't able to follow them to their hideout. How did you find it?"

"I . . . uh . . . Actually when I was looking for it, they kidnapped me."

"And took you with them?" Bunzo seemed skeptical. "Why would they do that?"

"Probably because I was too close to discovering their hiding place," said Seikei. True enough, he thought, since I was inside it.

"Take me there," said Bunzo.

"Oh, I'm sure they won't go back to it," said Seikei. "Now that they know *you're* after them."

"Perhaps," Bunzo said. "We could take a look, anyway. Where did you go while you were with them?"

"Just to a village up the coast."

"Would you recognize it?"

"I guess so." Seikei felt as if he were falling into a trap where he must either break his word to Captain Thunder or lie outright to Bunzo, and doing either would make him miserable. "They bought silk there," he offered.

"Chinese silk?"

Seikei shook his head. "No. I'm pretty sure it was silk made in the local area."

"Our information is that this gang has been smuggling goods from China. The shogun, as you know, is gravely concerned about such things. That was why he sent the judge to investigate."

Seikei thought he saw a way out of his dilemma. He could tell Bunzo the truth—well, part of the truth—and actually take some of the heat off Captain Thunder. Quickly, he explained the deception by which the gang had been buying goods from villages along the Inland Sea and passing them off in Osaka as Chinese.

Bunzo listened thoughtfully. "This throws a new light on the case," he agreed. "We must go back to Osaka Castle so you can report to the judge." He went to tell the helmsman to sail for the port. Returning, he said, "You shouldn't worry about delaying us. Now that we know who the smugglers are, we can find them again."

Seikei wondered if that were true. Captain Thunder also knew he had been spotted and would be wary about being seen in these waters anytime soon. "Maybe he'll make it to China after all," Seikei said absentmindedly.

"Who?" asked Bunzo.

"It doesn't matter. Listen, Bunzo, I can't go to the castle with you right now. You can tell the judge what I found out."

"What? But you must come. What could be more important—"

"I have to save a man from being executed," Seikei said. He explained why Ojoji had been accused of murder.

"Maybe he *was* the killer," Bunzo suggested. "Sometimes the correct answer is the most obvious one." Seikei smiled because he knew where Bunzo had heard that.

"I am convinced of his innocence," said Seikei. "But to free him, I have to find the real culprit."

"You know, this Judge Izumo is supposed to be a reasonable man," said Bunzo. "It wouldn't hurt you to flatter him a little."

"Bunzo!" Seikei could hardly believe his ears. "Compared to Judge Ooka, Judge Izumo is . . . is a—" Words failed him.

"I know that," said Bunzo. "But if you expect everyone to be like Judge Ooka, you'll be sadly disappointed."

Seikei saw the truth in this.

"How do you propose to find the killer anyway?" said Bunzo. The ship was within sight of the port now.

Seikei looked at the city, busy with boats, carts, and people, all rushing about in a way they seldom did in Edo. "Money," he said. "It must have to do with money. What else do the people here care about?"

"Perhaps it was one of the gang that kidnapped you," said Bunzo.

"No, it wasn't them," said Seikei. "They had an alibi both times."

"You're trying to figure this out the way the judge

would," Bunzo commented. "Why strain your brain? Come with me, tell him the story, and very likely he will identify the killer on the spot. Then I'll go with you and we can take him into custody."

Or her, Seikei thought to himself. "Bunzo, please," he said. "You must allow me to do this myself. I need to prove to the judge that I can handle it."

"And if you get killed," Bunzo said, "the judge will blame me."

"I won't," said Seikei, trying to sound confident.

"I'm not saying *I* would care," Bunzo added, "but—"

"I know, I know," said Seikei. "I don't think this person is dangerous to anyone but the members of the theater troupe."

"If you think that, you're definitely wrong," Bunzo said. "Remember, the judge says that anyone may become a murderer, given the right circumstances. But if the murderer kills a second time, that shows he's getting used to it."

"And each time after that it becomes easier," Seikei finished. "Yes, I remember. But Bunzo, I think you have also given me advice."

"What is that?"

"A samurai never fears death."

Bunzo frowned. "I'm not sure that will be comforting to the judge."

"I must do this," Seikei said. "I can't let Ojoji be executed."

Bunzo shrugged. "Go, then," he said. "But as soon as I have reported to the judge, I will come to the theater. Not that you would require my help."

"You've helped me many times, Bunzo," Seikei said. "Now you can help me prove I'm worthy of being a samurai."

As soon as the boat touched the dock, Seikei hopped ashore and headed for the Dotombori district. There was another reason why he didn't want Bunzo to accompany him. Seikei still was not entirely sure that his sister had had nothing to do with Nishi's murder.

What would he do if he found out she was guilty? His duty, of course, was to report the crime to Judge Izumo. It would be a test of Seikei's honor, his loyalty to the samurai code.

If Asako had been born a samurai, it would be easier. Confronted with proof of her guilt, she would be allowed to commit seppuku rather than face public disgrace.

That wouldn't work with Asako. Seikei still knew her

well enough to realize that. She would resist all the way to the executioner. He shook his head to chase the thought away.

He hailed a boatman and told him the destination.

"Come to Osaka for a little fun, eh?" the boatman said with a glance at Seikei's swords. Dotombori was widely known for its amusements of all kinds. The boatman, seeing that Seikei had come from the pier, assumed he had just arrived in the city. Seikei figured it was easier to allow him to think that.

"What puppet theater do you recommend?" Seikei asked.

"Till yesterday I would have said Takemoto," the man replied. "Chikamatsu wrote plays for the troupe there, you know. He was the best. A samurai too, they say." He winked at Seikei.

"But now they've closed," the man added.

"Trouble?" Seikei asked.

"More than a little, I'd say. The story is going around that a samurai—probably a ronin, not someone like yourself—became enraged and killed six people."

"That many?"

"Perhaps more," the man said. He lowered his voice, though no one else was near. "Jumped onto the stage and began flailing about with both swords."

"I'll make sure to avoid the place."

"Oh, you couldn't get in. Judge Izumo ordered it shut down. We're all safe as long as he's in charge."

"So I hear," said Seikei. He wanted to ask why Judge Izumo hadn't saved the six people—perhaps more—from the berserk samurai. He also realized he could get out of paying the fare if he revealed that the boatman's passenger was the dreaded killer. But at the end of the ride, Seikei quietly gave him the coin anyway.

Waiting for the boat to move on down the canal, Seikei walked up Dotombori Street to the theater. It certainly looked closed. Even the gaily colored banners out front had been taken down. It was a good time for Seikei to satisfy his curiosity about something. And he thought he knew a way to get inside.

At the edge of the canal he found one of the handy layered stones like the one he had used at his family's tea shop. He broke a thin slice off it and headed for the rear entrance of the theater.

18 —
THE SECRET OF THE STORAGE ROOM

Seikei let the door close behind him. The times he had been here before, the theater had been a hubbub of activity and noise. That made the utter silence that now pervaded the building even more eerie. Seikei had intended to find out just what was in the storage room that Kamori had the key to. But he wasn't sure exactly where it was.

All of the backstage rooms showed signs of having been abandoned abruptly. After Seikei left, Judge Izumo must have ordered everyone to clear out at once. Puppets—some partly disassembled—sat sprawled on worktables or in a heap on the floor. The musicians had taken their samisens home. But the black outfits of the puppeteers, along with some doll-size costumes, hung loosely from hooks along the wall and draped over furniture, as if the people and puppets who wore them had suddenly evaporated.

Gritting his teeth, Seikei forced himself to slide open the door to the head room. Once again he was confronted by a hundred pairs of staring eyes; odder yet, he had the feeling they had just turned toward the doorway to see who had entered. The sight sent a guilty shudder through him, as if the heads believed he was Nishi's killer, returning to the scene to gloat.

Nishi's own head, thankfully, had been removed. Seikei saw, however, that the blood on the floor had not been wiped up. Dried now, it bore the marks of footprints. Seikei stooped to look more closely. After Nishi's body had been discovered, people would have avoided stepping in the blood. It was an unclean spot. So any footprints must be those of the murderer. A tingle went down Seikei's spine as he thought of the scene. If only he could picture the man—or woman—who had stood here and made those prints.

An encouraging thought struck him. The footprints were too large to be Asako's. Her feet were small. The relief Seikei felt made him realize how much he had feared that his sister really had been a murderer. Of course, he reminded himself, she was still connected with the gang of smugglers—how deeply, he did not yet know.

After another moment's consideration, he realized

that the footprints didn't have the ridges that the high wooden clogs of a chief puppeteer would have left. Too bad that eliminated Sakusha as a suspect.

All at once, Seikei heard a laugh. He jumped to his feet, then realized it had come from somewhere else, not this room. But the most chilling thing about it was that it sounded exactly like Nishi.

As the echo of the sound died away, Seikei strained his ears to follow it. Had it just been his imagination? Or worse, did Nishi's spirit haunt the theater because no monks had come to clean and purify the place where he had died?

Seikei had been a little afraid of the head master even while the man was alive. The thought of meeting his ghost sent a chill through him. Maybe the laugh had been a signal that he should leave. Right now. Go ask Judge Ooka if he could intercede to save Ojoji. Since Ojoji was already in jail when Nishi was murdered, he couldn't have committed—

The sound of another laugh jolted Seikei's thoughts back to the present. This time it sounded as if it were coming from overhead. He looked up and saw only an ordinary ceiling. But he remembered that there was an upper floor to the theater. That must be where the storage space was that Ojoji had mentioned, the one that had caused an argument between Nishi and Kamori.

Seikei could see no possible entrance from this room. Hadn't Ojoji told him the staircase was in the prop room? That was right next door, so Seikei looked inside. The jumbled mass in here seemed worse than when he'd seen it before. But he spotted something that seemed new. There, at the far end of the room, was a set of stairs.

As he carefully made his way through the clutter on the floor, Seikei saw that the stairs were constructed to fold up. They fit into a hole in the ceiling and were probably not noticeable when closed.

He stood at the bottom and heard the laughter again. It was definitely coming from up there, from the black hole in the ceiling. And . . . there was no doubt it was Nishi's laugh. But how was that possible? With his own eyes, Seikei had seen Nishi's severed head. It was flesh and blood—still *oozing* blood in a way that no model maker, however skilled, could have imitated.

The only possible explanation Seikei could think of was that it was a ghost. He forced himself to think clearly, and then saw what should have been obvious. He was glad the judge was not here to see how long it had taken Seikei to realize what was staring him in the face.

Ghosts don't need staircases.

Whoever was up there was a person. A dangerous person, probably, as the killer of two people clearly must be. Seikei recalled his argument with Bunzo, and wished he hadn't been so insistent on coming here alone.

No. That was unworthy of a samurai. Once more Seikei reminded himself: A samurai does not fear death.

He grasped the hilt of his long sword and stepped onto the staircase. There was no railing, so Seikei had to concentrate on keeping his balance. One step farther up, then another. Now he could hear a voice, shrill, taunting, just like Nishi's. He stopped to listen, and as he did, another voice responded—deeper, slower. There were two people up there, perhaps more.

That considerably lessened the chances of their being ghosts. But it made it even riskier for Seikei to go up there alone. Now, only curiosity drove him onward. He was certain that he was about to discover the murderer.

Finally he reached the opening in the ceiling, where he could stick his head over the edge. What he saw was confusing. The upper floor was not divided into smaller rooms. Most of it was filled with boxes, racks of costumes, shelves with broken or discarded props, and scenery that had not been used for a long time. Dim light came through a few windows smeared with grit, but at the far end of the room stood a circle of candles, each one held inside a metal stand.

The scene was very dim from where Seikei stood, but he could see a large puppet seated on a raised platform, facing the ring of lights. And moving swiftly back and forth at the edge of the rings was another figure—this one human. The human was holding a second puppet, but of course with only one operator, the puppet's left arm and legs dangled lifelessly.

Realizing he hadn't yet been noticed, Seikei pulled himself up onto the floor. He squatted in the shadows, trying to locate the second person he had heard. The angry dialogue was still going on, and Nishi's laughter seemed more mocking than ever.

Suddenly Seikei saw the flash of a sword in the candlelight. He heard a cry of pain, and then saw something come rolling across the floor in his direction. Instinctively he reached to catch it. When he saw what it was, he stood up, slowly.

It was Nishi's head. Not the real head Seikei had discovered impaled on a pole. No, this was a puppet head, though the painted face was identical to Nishi's own.

The man on the other side of the room stood holding the now-headless puppet. He was watching Seikei. "I didn't know anyone else was here," the man said.

It was Takemoto. The theater owner who was also a skilled narrator. A man who took all the roles in the plays he narrated. There was no one else up here. The voices Seikei had heard had both been Takemoto's.

"I didn't want to interrupt you," Seikei said. He began to walk toward the man. "Go on with the performance."

"Oh, it's over," said Takemoto. Seikei saw a look in his eyes that hadn't been there before. By closing the theater, Judge Izumo had pushed Takemoto into a world of madness.

"I'm sorry I missed it," said Seikei. He held the head out to Takemoto.

"Nishi won't need that anymore," said Takemoto. He giggled, and Seikei realized he was once again imitating Nishi—quite successfully.

"Why did he lose his head?" Seikei asked. He noticed Takemoto was carrying a sword. It was a puppet-size sword, but the edge looked sharp.

"He talked too much," said Takemoto. "And he had done something bad. Very bad. He had to be punished."

"What was that?"

"The bad thing?" Takemoto looked around. Nobody was listening, except the puppet seated on the platform, but Takemoto's eyes seemed to see enemies in the shadows of the room. For a moment, he was so distracted that Seikei thought he would have to repeat the question. Then Takemoto, satisfied that they were alone, looked at him and said, "He killed Kamori."

Seikei thought Takemoto must, truly, be insane. "Nishi? Why?"

"Because Kamori fired his friend. They were very close. Both of them were strange. And also . . . because Nishi disapproved of Kamori for other reasons."

"When . . . How do you know?"

"I didn't know right away," Takemoto said. "But I was horrified when I learned Kamori had been killed. I wasn't sure if the theater could go on without him. That's why I let you investigate. You work for Judge Ooka, don't you?"

"How do you know that?"

"Kamori warned me. He had an informer in the castle who told him the judge was coming to investigate smugglers. And then here you were, asking questions. I thought you could find the murderer without disturbing . . ." Takemoto looked at Seikei without finishing his sentence.

"Without disturbing your role in the smuggling scheme?" Seikei asked.

Takemoto smiled.

"You wanted to make me think that Kamori was acting

against you," said Seikei. "But you knew about the smuggling scheme all along, didn't you?"

"I would have to, wouldn't you think?" said Takemoto. "It *is* my theater."

"Why did you tell me that you were the most likely person to have killed Kamori?"

"I thought that you would be impressed with my honesty, and not consider me a suspect as a result. I wanted you to think I was cooperating with you."

"How did you find out Nishi had killed Kamori?"

"He took me aside during the next day's performance. He was upset that we were going to continue using *The Five Men of Naniwa* play for . . ." He licked his lips and looked at Seikei with a cagey expression.

"I know that was how you signaled the smuggling gang."

Takemoto nodded. "Well, Nishi thought that we shouldn't. That he might object."

"Who might object?"

Takemoto gestured toward the puppet seated on a platform, the "audience," and lowered his voice as if the doll could hear. "Why, Chikamatsu, of course."

Seikei looked at the puppet more closely. It was, indeed, wearing two swords and old-fashioned clothing.

"This is Chikamatsu?" he asked.

"I hope you won't be like those who say that he's dead," said Takemoto. "You're clever. You must see that someone as great as he is will live on. Always. The only thing that changed was the receptacle for his spirit."

"Ahh . . ." Seikei tried to remember where the conversation had been going when it had been only slightly insane.

"So Nishi thought . . . Chikamatsu would object," Seikei prompted. "To what?"

"To using the theater as part of the smuggling scheme," said Takemoto, seeing Seikei's uncertainty.

"Because . . ."

"Because Nishi felt it dishonored the ideals of the theater."

"I see. So you killed him."

"Of course not. Do you think I'm like a daimyo who unsheathes his sword every time someone doesn't bow deeply enough?"

"No. But you must have had a reason."

"He would have told," Takemoto explained. "Told the authorities about the smuggling."

"Why didn't he tell me?"

"I was afraid he was going to. He enjoyed toying with

people, finding out what they were like. So I had to kill him before he decided to tell you. Fortunately your sword was just lying there."

"Yes, how fortunate," said Seikei.

"And now, I have reported everything to Chikamatsu. I dramatized it, just as it happened. And he approved."

"He did."

"Most definitely. Because, you see, if we didn't have the extra money that the gang and the merchants give us, we couldn't continue to operate the theater."

So it came down to the money after all, thought Seikei.

"Once Chikamatsu knew that, he told me I was right. For art is never adequately appreciated, you know."

"I know," agreed Seikei. "Do you know what I think you should do?"

"What?"

"Come with me so you can repeat the performance for Judge Izumo."

Takemoto looked wary. He was insane, but not insanely stupid. "I don't think he would appreciate it."

"He's quite an art lover," said Seikei.

Without warning, Takemoto lunged at him, wielding the sword. Seikei raised his arm and jumped out of the way, but the blade cut his wrist. Seikei looked down and saw blood. He drew his short sword, for it would be easier to use in close quarters.

"You're only making things worse," said Seikei.

"I can't let you go and tell everyone about the smuggling," Takemoto replied. "Chikamatsu wouldn't like it."

Takemoto made several more wild thrusts, but Seikei evaded them. He knew that all he had to do was allow his opponent to come close enough, and then run him through with the sword. Bunzo had shown him how to turn it so that it would slip between a man's ribs. "Go for the body," said Bunzo. "An easy target. On the left side where the heart is."

Somehow Seikei couldn't force himself to do it. Takemoto was a killer, true, but he was a pathetic madman. He should be brought to justice, but Seikei didn't want to play the role of executioner. However, waiting for Takemoto to tire himself out while trying to kill Seikei didn't seem like a good alternative. He might get lucky.

Then an idea came to Seikei. He kept moving to his left, making Takemoto follow him, until he was next to the puppet Chikamatsu. Quickly Seikei snatched it upright. Holding his sword to its throat, he shouted, "Put down your sword or Chikamatsu loses his head!"

Takemoto's face showed the horror he felt. "You can't!" he shouted.

"I will," Seikei threatened. "I know how. Drop it. Now."

Looking hopeless and defeated, Takemoto slowly let his sword fall to the floor. "All right," said Seikei. "Now we will all go to see Judge Izumo. All three of us."

Outside the theater, they met Bunzo, arriving to help, as he had promised. Seikei felt his face burn as Bunzo surveyed the situation. "I suppose there is some reason why you're holding your sword to the neck of a puppet?" he said.

"There is," said Seikei. But he knew that Bunzo couldn't wait to repeat the story that Seikei had used his sword to force a puppet to surrender.

19 —
JUDGMENT

*J*udge Izumo's courtroom was full. Shopkeepers and merchants from throughout the city knelt before him, heads bowed. Discarded scripts in the storage room had contained Kamori's notes on which merchants had dealt with the gang of smugglers and how much they had paid Kamori to change his scripts. Confronted with the evidence, all had confessed, and Judge Izumo was now handing down their punishment. Generally, this consisted of a fine, the size of which depended on the value of the smuggled goods each person had received.

Judge Ooka, Bunzo, and Seikei were observing the proceedings. When Seikei had delivered Takemoto (and Chikamatsu) to Judge Izumo, Judge Ooka was already there. He had arrived to discuss the case. They listened as Seikei explained everything that had happened, leaving out only a few details about the gang.

Bunzo had nudged Seikei at a certain point in the story. Forcing himself to do what Bunzo considered the wise thing, Seikei had given Judge Izumo credit for being the first to suspect Takemoto. In fairness, this was true, although Judge Izumo had more or less suspected anyone who didn't have an ironclad alibi.

Nevertheless, the compliment had pleased Judge Izumo so much that he had quickly released Ojoji and had also promised to consider another suggestion Seikei had made. Seikei was waiting now to see what he had decided.

The judge's assistant read the name: "Denzaburo, of Konoike Excellent Teas." Seikei's brother shuffled forward on his knees, trying to look as contrite and remorseful as possible. He was good at it. Even Seikei would have been convinced, if he hadn't heard from Asako that Denzaburo had bitterly blamed Seikei for causing all this trouble.

The judge reviewed aloud the case against Denzaburo and asked, "Do you confess to these crimes?"

"Yes, Your Honor," replied Denzaburo. "I don't know what possessed me to become caught up in this dishonest scheme. I can only plead that I was put in charge of the family business at a young age because my parents are infirm and ill and my older brother refused to accept the duties of running the business." Seikei gritted his teeth. Denzaburo was blaming *him*?

"Hm. Your older brother was adopted by a samurai, is that so?"

"Yes, Your Honor. A great thing for him, but it left a heavier burden on those of us who must work to support our aged parents."

"Is that so? You have an older sister, I understand."

"She is almost no help," Denzaburo said. "You know how women are. She wants to get married, and that is all she thinks about."

Judge Izumo nodded. "Well, since you have confessed freely, and saved us the trouble of using a torturer"—Seikei saw Denzaburo hang his head even lower at the thought—"I fine you two hundred *ban* for receiving illegally imported merchandise."

Denzaburo's body relaxed. He wouldn't enjoy paying the fine, but it was no worse than he had probably expected.

Then the judge said, "In addition . . ." and Denzaburo's body stiffened. Something he hadn't expected? What?

"I order you to provide the sum of four hundred ban to your sister Asako as a dowry. This will, I understand, be given to a husband she has already chosen."

Denzaburo slumped, reminding Seikei of a puppet that had been cast aside. The look of dismay on his face was genuine now, for certain.

"That will be all," the judge said. He glanced around, met Seikei's eyes, and gave the smallest of nods. Thank you, thought Seikei. Bunzo nudged him and Seikei got the message. All right, it had been a good idea to give Judge Izumo credit, deserved or not.

Two more days had passed, and Seikei was anxious to leave Osaka. He had been staying in the castle and had seen the famous Octopus Stone up close. But the days dragged by slowly because everyone in the castle was employed on some business for the shogun. Much of it seemed little different from running the tea business, except on a much larger scale.

Seikei wasn't eager to go out either. He had seen quite enough of the city and didn't want to meet Denzaburo by chance. In truth, since the smuggling case had been solved—except for finding the members of the gang, who were still at large—Seikei didn't see what was keeping the judge here.

Then he found out. "Fugu," the judge told him, rubbing his hands. "We're going to have fugu for dinner tonight."

"Oh, I forgot," Seikei said. "Father, I'm so sorry. I never obeyed your instructions to find a good restaurant that served fugu."

"You were very useful in other ways," said the judge. "In fact you really accomplished the task the shogun sent me here to do."

"Except capturing the smugglers," said Seikei. "I must tell you something," he added. It had been on his mind. "When I was with Captain Thunder and his gang, I gave him my word that I wouldn't betray him."

"Ah, so you held back some information. I thought your story was a bit sketchy in places. Did you, for example, neglect to tell us the location of their hiding place?"

"Yes," Seikei said. He was ashamed. What would the judge think of him?

"Actually, Bunzo found it," said the judge. "Your brother Denzaburo told us where to look. The gang has evidently abandoned it. Don't worry. I'm sure they are far away by now. Their crime really had more to do with tax evasion, which I am not responsible for enforcing. The shogun sent me to Osaka only because of the story that the gang was traveling back and forth to China. When you said that was false, you *were* telling the truth?"

"I'm sure of it," said Seikei. Though the captain had said otherwise, Seikei didn't believe him.

"Then I'm glad you kept your word of honor. Anyway, I'm indebted to your brother Denzaburo."

"For telling you where the gang's hideout was?" No doubt Denzaburo thought it was a good idea to curry favor with one of the shogun's officials. He was the type who liked to make friends in high places.

"That, and for another reason," said the judge. "It was *he* who invited us to the restaurant where we'll be eating fugu tonight."

Suddenly the dinner seemed much less appealing to Seikei. He trusted in the judge's wisdom, but had serious doubts about Denzaburo.

When they arrived at the restaurant, Seikei told Bunzo of his fears.

"You think it's possible your brother would try to poison the judge?" asked Bunzo.

"It's more likely that he chose a restaurant with a chef so incompetent he'll poison us all."

"Then we must take precautions to protect the judge."

Seikei agreed.

"When the fish is served, you take the first bite," said Bunzo. "I will observe, and if there is a bad reaction, I will execute both the chef and your brother."

Seikei blinked. "What . . . what kind of reaction will you be looking for?"

"Oh, choking, an alarmed look on your face. They say the reaction is quite swift. You probably won't suffer long."

"But . . . isn't there some other way to check the fish?"

"I can't think of any. You're not afraid of dying to protect the judge, are you? Because a samurai . . ."

". . . never fears death," finished Seikei. He just had the idea that he might face death by doing something more inspiring than eating a fish.

"After all, you managed to capture a puppet all by yourself," Bunzo said. "So eating a little fish should be child's play."

"I also captured a murderer, Bunzo," Seikei pointed out.

"To be sure. I give you credit," Bunzo replied.

Seikei was suspicious. If he hadn't known better, he would have sworn Bunzo was praising him.

Denzaburo welcomed them. He had reserved a private room, and they all sat on cushions around a table raised slightly off the floor. "This is a double celebration," Denzaburo said. "Two other guests will be coming. Let's have a little tea first." He poured from an earthenware pot. As Seikei tasted the hot liquid, he thought Denzaburo must indeed be celebrating, for this was high-quality tea. Not from China, perhaps, but from some place high up in the mountains where the growing season was short.

"Here are the guests now," Denzaburo said. Seikei looked toward the doorway and saw Ojoji and Asako enter. They looked happy, as well they should have, considering how things had turned out. But Seikei's attention was immediately caught by the garment his sister was wearing: a reddish-purple kimono with flying cranes embroidered on it.

Asako noticed Seikei staring and gave him a pretty smile. "Ojoji and I are engaged," she said.

"That's not all we're celebrating," added Denzaburo. "As you know, I was proud to provide a handsome dowry for my sister . . ."

Proud, thought Seikei wryly.

". . . and Ojoji has agreed to use the money to purchase a partnership in Konoike Excellent Teas."

Seikei's jaw dropped. "Wait. He's giving you back the money?"

Denzaburo smiled, pleased at Seikei's surprise. "Well, the theater closed and he has no job. So I offered to make him a partner in the business."

"He knows nothing about tea."

"He can learn. Anyway, Asako has worked for the business and knows a few things, so she can continue. There's plenty of room for the newlyweds to live upstairs."

Seikei shot a look at his sister. "Is this what you want?"

"We're going to be very happy," she said.

"And you have a new kimono," Seikei pointed out. He couldn't help himself.

"Yes, isn't it lovely?" she said. "A friend gave it to me."

So Captain Thunder returned to Osaka after all, thought Seikei. "I'm sure he wishes you well," he said.

Asako put her finger to her lips and gave him a look that said, *That's enough.* "He does," she said.

A waiter entered, bearing a huge covered tray. "Just in time," said Denzaburo. "Here's the fugu." The waiter lifted the cover of the dish to reveal a large round fish that had been gutted and filleted. He cut off a piece and placed it on a serving plate.

"Him first," said Bunzo in a voice that no one was likely to argue with.

The waiter set it in front of Seikei, who picked up a pair of ivory chopsticks. He took a small piece of the silver-white flesh and put it into his mouth. *Do it fast, without thinking,* someone had told him about the best way to commit seppuku.

He could hardly taste anything. The food he'd bought from a street vendor was more satisfying. He swallowed it without chewing. "Excellent," he said, bowing his head in Denzaburo's direction out of politeness. At least he had the satisfaction of knowing that if he died, Denzaburo would soon follow.

There was a pause. Seikei felt extremely self-conscious, aware that the others were waiting to see if he had a "reaction." He took a deep breath and then, just to annoy Bunzo, took a second piece of the fish.

"All right," Bunzo growled. "You may serve the judge now," he told the waiter.

Though Seikei found the fish disappointing, the judge did not. "This is wonderful!" he exclaimed after tasting it. "We'll have to return to Osaka for the wedding and eat here again."

Seikei and Bunzo exchanged glances. They were thinking the same thing: We must find some way to prevent that.

Authors' Note

Although the Japanese puppet theater is today called *bunraku,* that name refers to a nineteenth-century theater troupe. In Seikei's time, the early eighteenth century, it was known as *ningyo joruri,* meaning "doll storytelling." At that time, important developments were made in the puppets. The eyes and mouths of the dolls could open and close, and by 1733, the fingers could move to grasp objects. The three-man system of manipulating the puppets, still in use today, also originated about that time. Today, chief puppeteers—who are often famous stars—do not always wear the mask covering their heads, although the other two puppeteers customarily do.

In the 1700s, this kind of theater was particularly popular in Osaka, where the playwright Monzaemon Chikamatsu worked for the Takemoto Theater. Chikamatsu, born in 1653, died in 1725, and is today called the Shakespeare of Japan. (Of course, Japanese could call Shakespeare the Chikamatsu of England.) Chikamatsu liked to use contemporary events as the basis for his plays. This was particularly appealing to the people of Osaka, who were mostly low-class (but not low-income) merchants and shopkeepers. *The Five Men of Naniwa* is an actual play, and the five characters have the names we have used in our book. They are based on five gang members who were executed in 1702 and 1703. Afterward, their exploits became the subject of plays and stories, much like Robin Hood and his men.

Even today people in Osaka greet each other by saying, *Mo kari makka?* It means, "Making any money?"

As readers of our previous books know, Judge Ooka was a real person who became famous for his brilliance at solving crimes, and is known as the Sherlock Holmes of Japan. His adopted son Seikei is the creation of the authors.

Today, because of air pollution, you cannot see the Himeji castle from the Inland Sea, though Seikei could in 1737.